"The beauty of Ida Fink's spare and powerful stories is rooted in their subtlety, in those instants when the world shifts the smallest notch and things change or shatter forever."—*The Miami Herald*

"Beautiful, shattering . . . It is a tribute to this remarkable collection to say that it is very difficult and painful to read. . . . Here is one of those rare instances in which you feel honored and grateful for having a book made accessible in your own language."—*New York Newsday*

"Fink's stories skillfully elide the distinctions between fiction and nonfiction. They are acts of both reconstruction and deconstruction, reminding us that both the historian and the storyteller shape truth. . . . We're reminded once again of the conjunction between the sweetly ordinary and the profoundly extraordinary."—*The Philadelphia Inquirer*

"The stories are deceptively bare, but the impact deep."
— *Detroit Free Press*

"Philip Boehm and Francine Prose's translation is gentle and simple. Sentences exhibit the restraint and the degree of creative interpretation that mark fine translations. And Fink, whose heart must be broken in several places, reveals in these traces that it nonetheless still beats and listens."
—*Los Angeles Times*

"In all of these swift and sudden stories Ms. Fink exhibits a quiet fierceness . . . Subtlety and irony are her greatest tools, and she wields them well, tracing the arc of a mind in freefall, a world spinning wide apart."—*The Forward*

"Stark and moving . . . In her simple yet elegant prose, the writer tells tales that are the more touching and courageous for their focus on the ordinary gestures of people living through extraordinary times."—*Washington Times*

"Ida Fink's haunting stories—brief and unforgettable—lead us gently into the harrowing ordinariness of wartime Jewish Poland. Through the disturbing, painterly quality of her art we see them live again."—Johanna Kaplan, author of *O My America!*

"Ida Fink's work seems to me one of the best answers offered to the question of how the artist can confront the Holocaust. The delicate motions of consciousness are traced, in all their glorious subtlety, while the unspeakable forces of massed brutality come bearing down. Only a writer of the first rank could bring this off, and the world is lucky to have her.—Rebecca Goldstein, author of *Mazel*

ALSO BY IDA FINK

The Journey

A Scrap of Time

Traces

STORIES

IDA FINK

TRANSLATED BY PHILIP BOEHM

AND FRANCINE PROSE

AN OWL BOOK
HENRY HOLT AND COMPANY
NEW YORK

Henry Holt and Company, Inc.
Publishers since 1866
115 West 18th Street
New York, New York 10011

Henry Holt® is a registered trademark
of Henry Holt and Company, Inc.

Published in Canada by Fitzhenry & Whiteside Ltd.,
195 Allstate Parkway, Markham, Ontario L3R 4T8.

Library of Congress Cataloging-in-Publication Data
Fink, Ida.
[Short stories. English. Selections]
Traces: stories / Ida Fink.
p. cm.
ISBN 0-8050-4558-9
1. Fink, Ida—Translations into English. I. Title.
PG7165.I44A24 1997 97-6891
891.8'537—dc21 CIP

Henry Holt books are available for special promotions and
premiums. For details contact: Director, Special Markets.

First published in hardcover in 1997 by Metropolitan Books

First Owl Books Edition 1998

Designed by Debbie Glasserman

Printed in the United States of America
All first editions are printed on acid-free paper.∞

1 3 5 7 9 10 8 6 4 2

In memory of
my mother and father

CONTENTS

TRACES

THE END

They were still standing on the balcony, although it was the middle of the night and only a few hours kept them from dawn. Down below lay the dark, empty street; the trees in the square looked like black tousled heads. Once again it was quiet, too quiet after what had happened. From time to time a streetcar rumbled through the city center; a car rolled quietly past. The night was heavy, humid: one of those midsummer nights when not a single leaf trembles, and the asphalt, overheated during the day, exhales its steamy breath.

He slid his hand along the iron railing of the balcony and touched the girl's hand. Her hand was cold; she kept her fingers clenched.

"You see," he said. "It was nothing."

She wasn't looking at him, she was looking out over the roofs of the city, peering into the thick darkness; she sensed that he, too, was straining to listen. He said it was nothing, and yet he was listening.

"Don't be afraid, let's get some sleep." And again he said, "It was nothing."

"I'm not afraid," she answered loudly, angrily; her words spattered down onto the street like tiny, hurried footsteps. "And I'm not a child. Don't treat me like one. And don't lie to me. I can see that you're listening, too."

"But you are a child." He laughed. "My beloved little child . . ."

"Don't make me mad. And anyway—" She stopped in midsentence.

They heard a noise, at first far away, then clearer, close by—it was just a truck.

"Do you remember when we first realized that something was happening?" she asked, after the silence returned. Her voice was high-pitched and clear. The boy shut his eyes and thought, I love her, I don't want her to be afraid.

"Tell me," she insisted, "do you remember?"

"Of course. I could sing the exact moment for you, except you know how I sing."

"Don't joke now. This is an important night."

He put his arm around her; he could feel her body shaking. "It's an important night, love—because it's our night . . ."

In the darkness, he caught a glimpse of her angry expression. She was in no mood for either jokes or tenderness.

"I remember," he added hastily, and in an instant the music of that first moment surged inside him.

He recalled it exactly. The strings were growing quieter, preparing the way for the soloist. During the first measures of the larghetto, which he liked so much, he began to notice a faint buzz coming from the direction of the city. As if swarms of locusts were flying in from far away. Maybe not locusts, but simply the dense tremolo of the strings, rising to a forte, closer and closer, fleeing before the storm. The orchestra, which had once again picked up the piano theme, seemed muted, and the whole audience turned as if swept by a great wind toward the rumbling, now a loud and brutal thunder. He saw the pianist hesitate and watched his fingers attack the silent keyboard: by now, neither the piano nor the orchestra could be heard above the din. Then the tanks came rolling up the street alongside the park, their treads clanging and clattering. The storm crested and subsided. Once again it was quiet, and the full whisper of the strings reached the very last rows, where they were sitting.

"I remember," he said once more. "What an idea, to have a concert in the park!"

"Piotr," the girl whispered. She had never called him by his real name before, preferring instead the nickname Piotrus. "Piotr, think about it . . . three months of happiness . . . so little . . ."

For a moment he didn't realize she was talking about them; when he finally understood and tried to answer, the words stuck in his throat.

"And you go on insisting that nothing has happened. Why do you want to hide your head in the sand? People have been asking each other all week: When is it going to happen? Everyone knows that it is, that it's just about to . . ."

He managed to remain calm. "You're not making sense, you're upset. Look, the whole city is sleeping, all the lights are out. That proves that nothing has happened."

As if to spite him the darkness resounded with dull thuds. They raised their heads and listened. It was the same ominous music that had overpowered Chopin in the park. Tanks were once again riding down the city streets. Lights flickered on; voices could be heard through the open windows. She looked into his eyes.

"Let's go inside," she said.

She went back into the room and carefully locked the door to the balcony, as if she could lock out all the evil events of the night.

"Do you remember the first time I came here?" she asked, stopping in the middle of the room to look around. Piotr felt a chill run through him: Then, too, she had run into the room with rapid little steps, stopped still, and looked all around. Was she now unconsciously replaying that night?

"Do you remember? It was March, a very wet March, the snow was melting. Everything you were painting was green, and being in your room was like lying in the grass."

She was already looking back! Already recalling the past! He wanted to tell her, Don't say "was." Don't say: "You *were* painting." Say "is." Say: "You *are* painting."

"And you were playing Bach," he said.

"And I was playing Bach," she repeated. And added, "I'm so sad that it's already over."

"Stop it!" he shouted. "How can you say that! Nothing is over, we're still together, we're going to stay together. Always. Calm down. I'll make some coffee."

His hands were shaking. In the mirror he saw a pale face

that looked nothing like his own. The girl was saying, "Why lie? It's the end. The end of youth, the end of love, of your paintings, of my music. We were very happy, but there's no need to lie. Isn't it better to accept that we had three months of great happiness? And now they're over."

She met his gaze, read his answer. His face was chalk-white, taut with pain.

A low thrumming of windowpanes jarred her from her sleep. She bolted up in bed, wide awake, fully aware of what was happening. The room itself was now half dark; the windows had become glowing rectangles of gray. She waited. After a few minutes she heard a heavy, dull rumbling, as if the earth were sighing. The windows once again began to hum, but their music was immediately overwhelmed by a new explosion.

She glanced at her watch. It was almost four. Carefully, so as not to wake the boy, she moved over and leaned back against the wall. She watched him lying there, defenseless as a child and, like a child, unconscious of the evil that had been unleashed. She studied the rough darkness of his body, the hawklike profile of his young face. Gently she stroked his hair.

"Keep sleeping," she whispered.

She bent over him and stayed that way, keeping watch, guarding his last peaceful moments of sleep. The dawn advanced, followed by the sun. The war was fifteen minutes old.

THE THRESHOLD

The wooden porch was glassed in on all sides with huge panes. Until recently, curtains had hung in the windows, as yellow as the noonday sun. Not a restful color, but bright and warm; it complemented the nasturtiums that bloomed in the beds Mother tended all by herself. This year there were no nasturtiums either. Stripped of curtains and flowers, the front of the house looked strange and pathetic. Even these tiny changes showed how different things were now. The gate, usually latched with such care, hung by one hinge, lopsided, like someone about to faint. The windows were sealed tight, though it was the height of summer. The path in front of the house meandered toward the meadows and the river, past lush gardens and one-storied cottages. It was early morning, the beginning of July 1941, the first quiet, calm morning after days of intense worry. One week before, the Russians had fled the town. One week before, the Germans had marched in. The first pogrom had already taken place.

Elzbieta sneaked out onto the porch. It was cold; rivulets

streamed down the windowpanes. She sat in a wicker armchair—pale, but calm. She was thinking about her parents, whom the war had caught by surprise in L.; she wished that they would return as soon as possible. Once they came back, she thought, peace and order would return, too; everything would be the same as before . . . or almost the same. Elzbieta was still very young.

Every day she took Czing on his leash and went for a walk outside the town.

"It's safest by the river," she explained to Kuba. "The Germans never go down there—after all, these days there aren't too many Jews interested in swimming."

It was quiet by the river. The poplars glistened in the sun, gray-green, slender as columns; the water flowed lazily, covered with spreading blooms of gray spawn. The sand was hot.

They often stayed out the entire afternoon and went back just before dark, when the empty streets sighed with relief and fatigue after another long day. As they made their way through town, they could hear drunken voices coming from the bars, loud songs sung in a harsh foreign language.

"I never liked German even in school," she confessed to Kuba. "Now tell me if I wasn't right."

Kuba smiled and said nothing. He was much older; he knew more than Elzbieta, and had a better sense of the world. He put his arm around her and hugged her gently. She did not resist. It gave her a feeling of security.

"Let's go to the farmer's tomorrow to buy potatoes," she told him one day as they said good-bye in front of the porch. "I have to get them before my parents come back." At the thought of her parents she could hardly hold back her tears. Not now, maybe later, at night, when no one could see . . .

The next day they brought the potatoes in a wheelbarrow.

"Two sacks! That'll last a long time," she told Kuba happily. "We'll make pierogi and potato pancakes. Do you like pierogi?"

The furrow in Kuba's forehead disappeared when he heard her voice and looked at her young face, tanned by the summer sun.

Her aunts and uncle disapproved of her behavior. Elzbieta kept her distance from them, just as she distanced herself from their incessant concern with all the frightening and incomprehensible events. She locked herself in her own world and kept the others out. Even though they all lived under one roof, they hardly ever saw one another. Elzbieta refused to cross the threshold of their room, which seemed haunted by the spirit of that terrible time.

In vain they tried to reason with her, to explain things, to open her eyes, as they said. "Everything just slides off her like water off a duck! At a time like this, she wants to go walking. At a time like this."

The pastures smelled of chamomile and wild thyme. She lay next to Kuba on the trampled, fragrant grass, passing the hours.

"I just can't," said Elzbieta, "I just can't accept . . ."

Kuba took a box of tobacco out of his pocket, rolled a cigarette, and lit it.

"What can't you accept?" he asked.

She sat up and looked all around her, as far as she could see. The forest off to the east was slowly turning black. She saw herself in the meadow with flowers in her hair. She heard herself laughing. "Why are you laughing?" her teacher had asked at the school's spring outing. She hadn't wanted to say.

"What can't you accept?"

Instead of answering, she asked: "Tell me, Kuba, . . . you really love life, too, don't you?"

They walked along the riverbank, just as in the old days, down by the little beach, and then across to the pastures. They bought apples from the farmer and ate nothing else all day. In the evening Agafia made pierogi and put a steaming bowl of them on the table next to the window. Outside the window were lilacs, beyond the lilacs was the garden, and beyond the garden was the river.

Sometimes, when she lay awake in the darkness, she could make out bits of conversation coming from her aunts' room. Mostly cries and sighs. Then she would cover her ears with her pillow and burst into tears. Puzzled, Czing would lick her feet.

Two young SS men had been ransacking the house for over an hour. They stuffed their suitcases with the table silver, the kilims, the paintings, the porcelain. Elzbieta's uncle was at work; only the women were at home. When all their pleas were answered with harsh threats and warnings, the aunts took refuge in their room, but not even that room was spared. Since Elzbieta was the legal owner of the house, the Germans ordered her to assist with the looting, to show them around and explain where everything was. Nor did they overlook the attic, where they found the painting of a naked woman, which Elzbieta's parents had received on some occasion and stashed out of sight. They couldn't bear to look at it and only brought it out when the hapless person who gave it to them was about to visit. The SS men were very taken by the painting. They laughed as they used their riding crops to touch the breasts of the woman posed so nonchalantly.

Finally, when the whole house looked as if a battle had been fought there, they demanded a bottle of wine and two glasses. "I'll take it to them," Agafia whispered to Elzbieta.

Elzbieta sneaked out onto the porch. It was cold; rivulets streamed down the windowpanes. She sat there pale and very weary. "Come back," she pleaded with her absent parents. She could hear, from inside, the Germans' vulgar laughter and Agafia's angry mutter. A moment later she heard the sound of shattering glass; the Germans must have smashed the wineglasses. Then she heard steps. They were leaving. They shouted at her. She stood up, her back to the house, facing the shadowy street. *"Wo ist dein Vater?"*—"Where's your father?"—one of them remembered to ask. She didn't look at him. She focused on the spreading chestnut in their neighbor's garden.

"Dein Vater!"

"My father is at work," she lied, still looking at the tree. And at that moment she glimpsed something moving: A cat?

The first thing she noticed was the boyish face, the frightened eyes. How did he get here? A whole week after the fighting? And so young!

Then he emerged completely, his uniform in tatters, without a cap, his hair disheveled as if he had just woken up. He looked around. The little street was empty. She stifled a cry.

"Bitte," she said with effort, inviting the SS men back into the house. "There's still one more room. . . ."

"What?" shouted the older one. "Go have a look, Hans."

The Russian boy was approaching slowly; he seemed hardly able to walk. He was so close that she could make out the insignia on the uniform, the cuts on his hands.

"We've gone through the whole house," reported the younger one.

"Na, dann los!"—"let's go!"

They pointed to the bulging suitcases and instructed her not to touch them. They would be right back with the car. Then they headed for the porch door. She thought quickly, I have to stop them until he passes. I have to stop them.

"Bitte," she said shyly.

"Quiet!" the older one shouted, convinced that she was going to beg them not to take something.

Just in front of the porch, the Russian finally saw them. He ducked and ran.

The younger SS man cried out and chased after him.

"Come on." The older one pushed Elzbieta in front of him. "You will translate."

"They want to know where you were hiding," Elzbieta explained, her voice soft and kind.

"Schneller, schneller!"

The soldier didn't speak. Elzbieta couldn't bear to look into his eyes.

"Don't be afraid," she said, "I won't tell them anything, don't be afraid . . ."

The boy moved his lips and mumbled a few words. The only word Elzbieta understood was *zhizn*—"life."

"What did he say? Translate!"

"Let him go," she cried despairingly, *"ich bitte, ich bitte . . ."*

The older SS man peered at her. His eyes were sky blue.

"How old are you?"

"Fifteen."

"I'm twenty. And I've already shot seventeen people. This one'll be my eighteenth. Have you ever seen how it's done?"

She tore herself away with all her strength but then felt the strong arm of the SS man around her neck and something cold jabbing into her cheek.

"Schau mal—look, it's so simple. . . ."

The last thing she saw before she shut her eyes was the boy's final, bewildered gaze.

That evening she and Agafia buried him beneath the chestnut tree in their next-door neighbor's garden. Inside her aunts' room the light was already burning. A pot of kasha was cooking on their makeshift stove, filling the whole room with its aroma. Several people were sitting around the table.

"... and then they killed Goldman and his little son ...," her uncle was saying quietly.

Elzbieta crossed silently into the room and took her place at the table.

ALINA'S DEFEAT

Shortly after the Germans occupied the city, Alina's boyfriend asked her to go to his house and sound out his landlord—discreetly, so as not to arouse suspicion—about whether the Germans or Ukrainians had been asking for him and, if they had, whether they had searched his room. Alina's boyfriend was a journalist and the author of several fiercely anti-Nazi articles.

This was a big favor to ask. In those days every threshold led to the unknown, or rather to some disaster of an as-yet-unknown nature. Of course the four walls of a room hardly guaranteed protection. Still, they gave the illusion of security—which was no small matter.

After hearing Antoni's request, Alina got up from the sofa where they had both been resting after their midday meal (for two weeks they had been eating potatoes sprinkled with sugar: Antoni provided the potatoes; Alina had a stock of sugar) and went to the mirror to put on some makeup. Lately, whenever she left the house—and she had done so two or three times—she always made up very carefully, with mascara and rouge, and dressed elegantly. This painstaking attention to her appearance was designed to deceive the eye.

As she was applying her makeup, she noticed she was very pale and that her hand was shaking.

"Is it really necessary?" she asked as she kept brushing on mascara. "So what if they were there? You're still not going back. From now on you're staying here with me."

"It's necessary," Antoni replied. "But since you don't feel up to it"—he didn't say, But since you're afraid—"don't go. Karolowa said things were quiet today," he added, referring to the maid.

"What do you mean!" exclaimed Alina. "Of course I'm going. Don't forget, just the day before yesterday I went to see Irena. I simply strolled on over, just like that, calm as could be. I'll be ready in a second."

Suddenly she was energetic, even cheerful. It was hard to say what had changed her mood: Karolowa's observation or Antoni's suggestion that she didn't "feel up to it." In her excitement she forgot that Irena's was just down the block, whereas Antoni's house was at the other end of the city.

Of course I'm going, she thought, rubbing rouge into her cheeks. I'm sure no one's been around to check, but he won't calm down until I tell him they haven't been looking for him.

She put on her light blue dress, her dark straw hat, and gloves.

"You look beautiful," said Antoni, and then, "I can't go there myself, and besides, I don't look like just one Jew—I look like three! Like hundreds, like a whole tribe!"

"Let's not exaggerate," Alina replied gaily, "either about my looking so beautiful or about your being a whole tribe of Jews."

Her landlady stopped her in the hall. "You're going out? That's crazy. It was quiet this morning, but my daughter just called—"

Alina smiled politely and quickly closed the door behind her. It was a sunny, lush afternoon. The chestnut trees cast their shadows on the sidewalk; fragrant flowers filled the windowsills. Far away, at the end of the street, a streetcar rang its bell.

At first she walked lightly, easily, but once she reached the square, where several streetcar lines crossed and where she met the first passersby, she felt the muscles in her legs begin to tense.

In two hours everything will be over and done with; I'll come back, sit down on the sofa, and tell him how my calves started to cramp. And she walked on, refusing to slow down, even though she was afraid.

She decided to walk the whole way. Neither she nor Antoni trusted the streetcars, which in any case only went as far as the Polytechnic. After that she still had a long distance to go before she reached Antoni's house.

The city was silent and motionless after the bloody storm that had so recently raged through its streets and houses. The deathly calm was charged with terror; the nerve-racking silence suggested imminent ambush; it grated on the nerves. The deeper she pushed into the city, which was so empty it seemed naked, the more she began to panic.

She walked on, reluctantly, full of growing anger at Antoni; the whole expedition suddenly seemed ridiculous, the result of his fevered imagination.

She was close to tears. She told herself she was a fool to continue. Writhing with fear, she walked on.

In this way she covered half the distance and turned onto the wide, shaded ulica Pelczynska, where the Gestapo had set up its headquarters. The street had become much more than just a street; it was an entire concept. When people said, "They were taken to Pelczynska," no further comment was necessary.

Wrapped in her fear, and waging a mental argument with Antoni about the senselessness of her mission, she hadn't even noticed which street she had taken.

All of a sudden she stopped dead in her tracks. Fifty meters away, trucks blocked the street. A few Gestapo officers were buzzing around the entrance to a building. A small group of people had just disappeared behind the gate. Germans walked back and forth. Trucks were driving away.

"What is it? A roundup?" Alina asked a boy who had just passed the Germans and was walking on calmly.

"They're checking papers, but not everybody's. Just people they don't like. In your case"—the boy looked at her admiringly—"there's obviously no need to worry."

Of course not. I'll just stroll right by without a care in the world.

But she couldn't move. She stood there helplessly, struggling with herself. Another truck drove up, and another group of people disappeared behind the gate; Gestapo officers kept moving back and forth on the sidewalk.

She stood there a long time. Finally, she gave up.

She turned back and headed home. Her fear evaporated; she was no longer afraid. All she could think about was her defeat and how she would face Antoni and what she would say to him. Her despair assumed gigantic proportions—just as her fear had a moment before—and for a minute Alina wondered whether she wouldn't have been better off if they had caught her.

When she walked into the room, Antoni jumped up from the sofa and asked, "Were they there?" His impatience and his eager expression sapped what was left of her strength.

"I never got there," she said. But he mistook what she was saying for, No one's been there, and his face brightened.

"I never got there."

"You never got there? You couldn't get through? Things were starting up again?"

"I made it as far as Pelczynska, and I couldn't go any farther. They were checking papers in front of the Gestapo headquarters. I wanted to keep going. But I couldn't."

Antoni bit his lip and said, "It's a good thing you didn't. You might not have made it back."

"I'll go again tomorrow," she said, in a pathetic effort to save face.

"Let's see how things are tomorrow. Maybe we'll go together. Maybe I'll go by myself. Don't worry. Don't think about it."

The evening passed in silence. Antoni read a book; Alina went into the kitchen to cook her potatoes.

"You made it!"

Karolowa was sitting by the stove, as always, eager to chat.

"The landlady said you went into town. Things were quiet in the morning. But then they started rounding people up. On the market square and across the river. It's a good thing you made it. Is Pan Antoni staying overnight? Where's he going to sleep? There's only one bed in your room."

"I guess he'll have to sleep with you," Alina snapped back.

At supper Antoni lectured at great length on the architecture of Romanesque churches in France. Alina choked down the sweetened potatoes and thought that things would never be the same. It shouldn't be like this now, she thought, just when we ought to be closer than ever.

She was the first to go to bed. Antoni took a long time splashing around in the bathroom.

"War's war and shame's shame," she heard Karolowa judging her in a voice intended to carry throughout the apartment.

"Did you hear her?" Antoni was laughing as he came out of the bathroom. "Are you ashamed?"

I should have gone on, I should have gone on, she was thinking.

She lay awake listening to the town-hall clock strike one hour after the other. She didn't fall asleep until dawn.

She dreamed she was walking down the street. A young German blocked her path and shoved her into the entranceway of a Romanesque church. The German had the face of the boy who told her she had no need to worry. They caught me, she thought joyfully, and for one brief moment of sleep, she was at peace.

ZYGMUNT

It was the beginning of June 1941. Final exams had already started, and we would meet by the swimming pool next to the park to discuss our assignments in counterpoint and harmony—our satchels contained bathing suits as well as sheet music. The sunlight played on the chlorinated water, and everything was green, so that we wondered what key went with sunshine, and what key went with green.

There was Franka, with her wide, flat face and fantastic legs, a lover of Bach and jazz; Rysiek the composer, fine featured and slim; and Ala. All three were killed a few months later.

But this is not about them; it's about Zygmunt, a small, inconspicuous boy from some far-off, provincial place—a little arrogant, a little unpopular. He used to visit me now and then, so that Pani H., from whom I rented a room, was convinced he had a crush on me. And although I don't think that was true, I do think that Zygmunt desperately craved friendship, which he could never seem to find because of his distant, standoffish personality. He was one year ahead of me; he worked hard and spent entire days practicing the piano. The program he was working on for his graduation recital was long and difficult. I promised him more than once that I would drop by and listen to him play. He was hungry for applause and acclaim, but I was busy with exams and even more so with love. So I kept putting the visit off from day to day.

By the time I managed to see him, people were already talking openly about war. Zygmunt's room was small and tastefully furnished—books, pictures, flowers—he was a bit pedantic, with a highly developed aesthetic sense. I sat down on the sofa bed and listened to him play Beethoven's Third Concerto. He performed it very well; his long, flexible fingers had impeccable technique—assured and powerful. But without, as they say, heart. When he finished, I told him everything sounded fine. He seemed pleased.

A few days later the war arrived, and I discovered the fear of bombs, but that soon seemed childish and silly compared with what came next: the fear of people.

Trucks covered with tarpaulins sped through the streets of the city hauling the Jews away to some unknown destination. Death became an everyday event; people spoke about it matter-of-factly as they stood in line for bread; fear became a natural state. Inside the houses, the walls resounded with the first rudimentary words of a new language: *aufmachen, raus, los.* Appearances changed; people's eyes looked different, their faces, their lips.

I ran into Zygmunt. He, too, looked changed. He told me that three weeks earlier they had dragged him from his apartment. He thought that was it—but no, he was working outside town now, leveling ground for an airport they were building. When I told him how lucky he was, he just smiled at me, faintly, oddly.

We parted quickly. Who had time or patience for friendly chats in those days? Who cared about anybody else? We were all egoists.

Some time later I found myself in his neighborhood. I was dead tired after scouring floors in the town hall—the happy outcome of a street roundup. I was in great need of music.

No one answered my knocking. I called out, "Open up, it's me." I turned the doorknob.

The room was half dark. The curtains were closed. Zygmunt lay on the sofa. He didn't get up to greet me. In fact, he didn't even move. In a muffled voice he invited me in, "Come in, come in," and continued lying there without speaking.

"Did I wake you up?"

"I wasn't asleep."

"I was passing by and thought I might get you to play something for me. But I don't want to bother you. I'll come back some other time."

I was already on my way out when he jumped up from the bed, took a seat at the piano, and opened the keyboard. Without taking time to concentrate or collect his thoughts, as musicians usually do, he immediately started playing as if it were extremely urgent; the two brief passages in C minor sounded like a cry.

I shuddered, suddenly cold. There was nothing distant in that playing, nothing artificial. It was pure music welling up from the depth of his soul. I forgot about everything and listened raptly to Beethoven's Third Concerto.

Zygmunt finished the first movement, waited until the last note died away (he was still a bit pedantic). Then instead of playing the soft E-major chord that begins the second movement, as I expected, he turned to me and said:

"You know, they beat us there very badly."

It took me a minute before I understood. I didn't know what to say. I was afraid.

"Very badly," he repeated. "They kick us. Look."

He opened his shirt and showed me his chest; in the half dark I could hardly see anything.

"So why do you go there?"

He was silent. He sat leaning forward, holding his head in both hands.

"At first there were twenty of us," he said after a moment. "Now there are fourteen."

"And the others?"

"Every single one . . ."

"Don't go back!"

"They wrote down where we live. They'll come after me."

"Maybe they won't. Don't go."

"Every day I tell myself, Don't go. Take a chance. And every day I go back. Before you came I was lying down thinking about how they were going to beat me tomorrow."

"Zygmunt!" I shouted. "What's the matter with you? Get a grip on yourself! Do not go back!"

"You're right, you're right. But I just can't seem to. . . ."

"Zygmunt," I said, this time quietly and calmly. "Do something, defend yourself, do you hear me? You have to do something. . . . You have to. . . ."

He smiled. Like a grown-up might smile at a child's silliness.

Zygmunt did not survive. I don't know when he was killed, or where. We were never all that close, and I confess that after the war, when I heard about his death, I received the news with a vague, distant sorrow. So many close, dear friends were claiming my tears.

AN AFTERNOON ON THE GRASS

We were sitting on the grass, Natalia, Masha, and I, beneath a cherry tree heavy with dark, sweet fruit, in a dense, sheltered orchard. In the middle of the orchard stood a small, modest cottage where, by the time we came to visit, Natalia's parents had been renting a room for two months.

Their former house was located on the town's main street; it was dark and full of heavy furniture. There, everyone used to speak very loudly, because Natalia's father was deaf. But here, in the cottage, both Natalia and her mother spoke in a whisper—though her father's hearing was, of course, no better. I was astonished to hear the low murmur of the usually loud voices and to see the deaf old man smiling stiffly, embarrassed by the silence that streamed from the moving lips wherever he turned. He was playing with the chain of his pocket watch, passing it through his fingers like a rosary, and gently nodding his head. His face was still kind, just as I remembered it from the days when his family would shout themselves hoarse to allow him into a world closed off by his deafness. The murmur was uncanny, this whispering around a man already immersed in deafness, ignored—and blissfully ignorant.

"Is it quiet in town?" Natalia's mother asked in her muted voice. "What's going on? Are things quiet?" Her father pointed to the orchard and exclaimed, "Look at the garden we have here—how green everything is."

Natalia's mother seemed gloomy and worried. Gently but firmly, she pushed her husband across the threshold into the cottage and shut the door behind him. Then she asked again, "Is it quiet? Really quiet?"

Natalia sat silently, her head bowed. Her neck had broken out in a rash, just as it had after her graduation exams. With her bangs cut straight across her forehead and her freckled nose, she still looked like a well-behaved schoolgirl. She had been the quietest girl in class, and it wasn't until the final exam that she had surprised everyone with her written essay, "Landscapes in Polish Literature." The school principal, a teacher of Polish literature, pronounced the essay excellent. Peering at Natalia as if he were seeing her for the first time, he said, "You absolutely must go on to the university and study Polish literature."

Natalia's neck reacted to the principal's praise by breaking out in red splotches, but her best friend, Masha, who was standing next to her, snorted with laughter. "*Panie dyrektorze,* you've got to be joking! A Jewish girl studying Polish literature at the university!" Masha was bold and outspoken, totally different from quiet Natalia, who after that fleeting triumph did indeed move to the nearby town, with its famous university—to take courses in dressmaking. She cut and sewed for exactly a year, then the war broke out. I also left for the nearby town and returned a year later. Only Masha the bold, the mocking, didn't go anywhere, because her family had no money. She worked as a private tutor.

Now the three of us were sitting in the dense orchard beside the poor peasant cottage to which Natalia's parents had moved, hoping that this move would save them from disaster. All the exams, all the departures, all the return trips home, were far behind us, in a world that had ceased to exist. Which is why neither Natalia nor myself understood, at first, what Masha meant when she said, "I envy you that year. I never envied anyone before. But now I envy you."

Natalia's mother appeared on the doorstep with a plate of pancakes made with dark flour. "They're for you. Go on and eat," she said, and once again asked, "Is it really quiet in town?"

Natalia looked at her imploringly. "Mama, please, Mama." Touching her raw, burning neck, she explained in a whisper, "Mama's always asking whether things are quiet in town. As if that meant anything. She never used to be like that. She was always even tempered and reasonable."

"None of us is like we used to be." Masha cackled loudly. We didn't recognize that cackle. The pancakes were chewy and tasteless; we could hardly eat them.

"What was it you said a minute ago?" Natalia asked. "Why do you envy us?"

"I was saying that I envy you that year, the last year before the war, when you were away. That year that you spent by yourselves. New places, new faces."

"I don't know what you mean. I've already told you how many times I just wanted to give up and go back home. Sewing classes—how boring. Obviously you have the wrong idea."

"I know exactly what I mean," Masha interrupted, annoyed, "and she"—here she pointed at me—"knows what I mean too."

I thought that probably I did, but I didn't say anything, I didn't even look at Masha; I just stared out across the flat plain over which the sun was setting. The sky was turning red, the windowpanes had taken on the color of the sweet cherries. And looming in the window was the kind face of Natalia's father. He was gesturing to us with his hands.

The door of the cottage suddenly flew open, and Natalia's mother rushed out. This time she didn't ask us anything; she didn't say a word—she just ran to the gate, propped her elbows on the wooden fence, and stood there for a long time facing town.

"I thought I heard some shouts," she said, coming back. "But there's nothing. Everything's quiet."

The glow of the kerosene lamp lit the inside of the cottage. Natalia's father opened the window and called out, "Aren't the mosquitoes bothering you, girls?"

"Mosquitoes, mosquitoes." His wife sounded exasperated. "He's worried about mosquitoes."

Masha leaned toward me with her flat dinner plate of a face. Her eyes searched out mine.

"They say you had a boyfriend there. Is that true?"

"It's true."

"Tell me. . . . Is it really so beautiful? . . ."

"Masha! How can you!" Natalia exclaimed.

"We'd better be heading back," I said, and Masha stood up obediently.

Natalia accompanied us to the road. The evening was cool. Fog was drifting in over the fields. We walked back quickly. A small boy ran by us shouting in Ukrainian, *"Zydiw bijut"*—"Hurry, they're beating Jews"—and smiled, pleased at his joke.

The town was silent. Just past the bridge, before we went our separate ways, Masha stopped. In the darkness her face shone, white as a mask.

She said, "Don't be angry. Please understand, I'm just so sad that . . . I'll never know . . . that I'll die without ever . . ."

I turned onto our street and ran. I could see the pine trees in front of our house, darker than the dark, and while I was running I thought, Poor, poor Masha, and when I reached the door, I pressed the bell with my finger and rang in a frenzy, so that I could open the drawer as quickly as possible and take out the letters I knew by heart and read them and read and read . . .

A CLOSED CIRCLE

The truck passed the last houses of the city and drove onto the empty highway. The asphalt was damaged, plowed up by the caterpillar treads of tanks; the trees lining the road were broken, bent in two. But it was enough to look past the ditch that ran alongside the road to find the old prewar world. The fields and meadows remained unchanged. The rising sun illuminated the stubble, buttercups shone yellow in the grass, and mounds of white daisies looked like patches of snow left behind by winter.

Jozef sat facing the fields and meadows. The sight of the greenery and flowers had an unexpected effect on him (he was generally immune to nature's charms), an unexpected, soothing effect. For the first time in many years—longer than he could remember—he was overcome by the desire to lie down in the shade of a tree and breathe deeply. This was particularly odd considering that Jozef, an accountant formerly employed by a leading import firm, had long since passed forty and had never in his orderly, industrious life been prone to bouts of sentimentality. It was difficult even to imagine his somberly attired slim body, lolling beneath a pear or an apple tree. He seemed better suited to cobble-stone streets and city cafés than to stubble fields and daisies. Even so, he would have bristled at anyone who found his reaction odd. He was convinced that he had long been yearning for green fields and shady groves, just as he was now, as he bumped and bounced down the war-torn highway, precariously perched on his suitcase in the back of the truck. He was fleeing to his native town, which he had left for good twenty years before, and which he now visited only once a year, during the holidays, to see his parents.

None of the other passengers paid any attention to the world beyond the roadside ditch. The men were playing cards, and the one girl, who was sitting propped up against the cab of the truck, had her eyes closed. Despite the fact that he hadn't exchanged a word with her, Jozef felt they were connected by a common fate. The men, on the other hand, were returning from what they called business trips; their crates and packages contained stolen goods. Their faces were red and swollen; though it was still early, they were drinking heavily. Their card game was punctuated by drunken, raucous shouts.

Before their departure Jozef had exchanged a few words with one of the men as he paid the exorbitant price for this trip to Z.—many times the cost of an ordinary train ticket. But that was not what they had talked about: the price was not negotiable. Not only were you expected to pay it, you were also supposed to be grateful for the chance to make this illegal trip. Jews were not allowed to leave the city without a pass—but no passes were ever issued.

The man whom he was paying for the trip, the scion of a well-known family of petty thieves and rowdies in Z., had peered at Jozef and asked if he wasn't the son of that bearded man who owned the shop next to the parish church. When Jozef answered that he was, and asked if his parents were all right, the man said, Well, they're still alive, if that's what you mean. Then he took a flask of vodka from his pocket and offered Jozef a drink. When Jozef refused, he continued with a loud laugh: *"V Z. teper* ya *korol"*—"Now *I* am king of Z."

Jozef had scrambled up the ladder and sat on his suitcase. He hadn't believed he was actually going to escape from the city until he heard the driver start the motor. He didn't see the girl get on; when he first noticed her, she was already sitting in the truck, propped against the cab, and her eyes were closed. Her black, tightly curled hair, her large eyes, so visibly prominent now that her eyelids were drawn smoothly over them, made everything perfectly clear. Is she from Z.? he wondered. But a moment later he stopped thinking about her. In fact, he stopped thinking altogether.

Lately this had been happening often. He seemed to lose himself in thought, to fall into a reverie; he suffered from lapses of consciousness, and his mental paralysis was invariably accompanied by physical paralysis. It would begin with an unpleasant feeling of tumbling into an abyss (as sometimes happens in a dream); the feeling passed once the fall was over. Then an empty space would open up, a vacuum, and Jozef, suddenly weightless, would hang suspended in the void, with no desire, no desire at all, to climb out. These attacks (or lapses, as he called them) wouldn't have bothered him were it not for the fact that they usually happened at very inconvenient moments, times when he most needed to think quickly and efficiently. So this falling into a vacuum was actually extremely dangerous.

The first time, it had happened in broad daylight, on a street blocked off by a green wall of helmets and uniforms. The situation was grim but not hopeless, since the entrances to the buildings lining the street were open; the simplest defense was to hide in the dark interiors of the stairwells—although this was not foolproof, as it turned out. In any event that is what many of the passersby caught in that ambush did; the crowd thinned rapidly until the only people left on the street were those who ran no risk of dangerous complications when they presented their identity papers.

Jozef had remained outside in the open, despite the stamp on his identity card, despite his face and the white armband on his sleeve, with its carefully sewn six-pointed star. Despite, one might say, common sense. Of course, the hunt wasn't limited to the street; the helmeted hunters carried out a meticulous search of the stairwells, basements, and courtyards, so that they bagged most of those who had hidden and who, along with Jozef, were marched off to forced labor in the building that had served as Gestapo headquarters for the last month. When the job of washing floors and hauling furniture was completed, those who had been working on the ground floor were let go, while those who had performed the same job on the upper levels were detained. Just as Jozef, in his wet clothing, his face scored by a riding crop, was crossing the street, five trucks full of men in helmets and uniforms drove into the yard. They were singing a melodious song. Their voices were strong and youthful and harmonized well.

Jozef realized that the bewilderment and momentary paralysis that had first overcome him during the street roundup and had plagued him repeatedly ever since had nothing to do with cowardice or with what is commonly called losing one's head. It was more complicated than that: a question of mysterious forces whose existence he had never before suspected.

After the incident with the picture he decided to consult a doctor.

The cheap reproduction of a Brueghel—which hung in a heavy gilded frame in his rented room—nearly caused a disaster. During one of the visits that the helmets and uniforms paid to the armbands with the six-pointed stars, there appeared in Jozef's room, accompanied by the obliging wife of the caretaker, a personage in a uniform and helmet who was, as it turned out, an art lover. This passion changed the course of the visit completely. Having noticed a porcelain figurine of Leda and the Swan, the personage in the uniform momentarily forgot his real reason for coming and pointed at this piece of china kitsch with his leather-gloved hand. Jozef handed it over compliantly, then opened a drawer and took out several similarly kitschy porcelain and bronze statuettes. These were the pitiful remnants of his deceased aunt's small shop. It was only out of respect for her memory that Jozef had not thrown them into the trash. The men in uniform ordered Jozef to *einpacken*, and Jozef, who did not have a work card, gladly obeyed. The art lover was on his way out when the picture, hanging in a corner, caught his eye. He appraised it with a professional interest, squinting slightly, then without a word nodded his helmeted head. It was then, just as the visit was coming to such an unusually happy end, that the mysterious, gloomy forces stirred in Jozef. He plunged into his void, losing all awareness of time and place, and couldn't lift a finger. *"Los!"* the personage in the helmet barked—"move"—and again, louder, more threateningly, *"los!"* but this time, too, with no effect.

The fact that Jozef had managed to run away from the plaza in front of St. Magdalena's Church bordered on a miracle. Shortly afterward a long line of trucks covered with tarpaulins set out from there.

After this happened, he was terrified by the forces that, he realized, would surely lead to his destruction. He considered looking up a doctor he knew from a weekly chess game in a café; the mental effort and concentration demanded by that game had always precluded casual conversation. If they finished playing before six o'clock (when both left the café and headed off in different directions), they discussed the latest plays of the grand masters or the most interesting endgames. Although this was the extent of their acquaintance, Jozef considered the doctor to be one of his closest friends—he only had one other, a lawyer, whose love for music was especially appealing. Jozef often went with him to orchestra matinees. Jozef valued his friend's knowledge of music but was a little put off by his overly romantic taste. He could not, for example, forgive him for idolizing Verdi and Puccini, whom Jozef, a lover of Bach and Mahler, regarded with contempt. Also the lawyer had an annoying habit; when he left the concert hall, he hummed whatever composition he had just heard, and this noisy testimony to his intimacy with music (as well as his sonorous bass voice) grated on Jozef. He felt closer to the doctor–chess player.

Of course, he had other relationships, but they were transient and inconsequential. He remained a confirmed bachelor.

The doctor wasn't in. His two children stared at Jozef in terror.

"They took my husband away a week ago," said the wife. She didn't ask Jozef to sit down, but he didn't blame her. He left. A troop of soldiers was marching down the street. The soldiers were singing this time, too; again they had strong, youthful voices that harmonized well. *Und morgen die ganze Welt* . . .—"and tomorrow the whole world!"

He began walking toward the neighborhood at the edge of town where the lawyer lived. But then abruptly he stopped and turned back.

His landlady, who had been renting him the room with the Brueghel reproduction for years, was waiting for him in the hall. He listened to her without interrupting. Somehow he understood that this terrified woman was evicting him for her own safety and peace of mind.

Toward evening he dragged himself from the couch and

stood by the window. A blue fog hung over the town. The town-hall spires loomed like some strange orchard against the rays of the setting sun. A trolley car climbed a steep hill. Silence fell on the plazas and squares and on the deserted streets he knew so well.

While he stood there, contemplating the town and the life he had spent there, he heard a muffled cracking, like a scaffold collapsing, far away. Perhaps twenty years of a different life, a life marked by storms, by soaring flights and violent crashes, by all sorts of strong emotions—perhaps such a life would come tumbling down with a thunderous roar. But Jozef's life, as pedantic and orderly as the drawer with the porcelain kitsch, could manage only that distant, muffled thud.

The landscape floating by on both sides of the highway succeeded in coaxing Jozef out of his trance. His initial intoxication had passed, but a kernel of euphoria remained inside him, ready to burst open at any moment. Though not here, not now. The men had finished playing cards and were discussing recent events so loudly and so crudely that it was hard for Jozef to ignore their shouts and raucous laughter. His willed deafness required great effort. He tried returning to his comforting void, but now, ironically, when he most needed it, it was inaccessible. All he wanted was not to think, not to hear, not to know. Why? He wasn't one to waste time looking for reasons. In any case, there were too many reasons, not the least of which was the recent cracking of that scaffold.

As the men continued their discussion, the face of the girl leaning against the cab of the truck grew paler and paler until at last it seemed transparent; Jozef's face remained unmoved, calm and peaceful. In fact, as the narrative unfolded, cruel and brutal in its details, the kernel of euphoria actually swelled. Jozef puckered his lips and began to whistle—a pure, high tone. And it's hard to say what was more remarkable, the tune itself or the sheer fact that he was whistling for the first time in ages. He himself would have been astonished to hear what he was whistling—the same hackneyed aria from *Rigoletto* that his lawyer friend liked so much; not Bach, not Mahler! But he didn't hear, he didn't know, and only the girl's stare and the sudden silence made him aware that he had committed a faux pas. The girl looked at him with surprise and distaste, and the silence was broken by the men's laughter.

"Go on, whistle," they said to him in Ukrainian. "You won't be whistling long." One way or another, he'd achieved the desired effect. The operatic intermezzo put an end to the stories; a new card game began, and a bottle of vodka appeared. The girl kept staring at Jozef. Tiny wrinkles creased her forehead, and her head sank between her shoulders. She looked like a terrified blackbird.

Jozef reached into his pocket, took out his cigarette case, and lit up. He considered smoking to be a harmful pleasure and indulged only at moments of intense emotion, during particularly stressful chess games, for example, or after a good, "uplifting" (as he liked to say) concert.

Today the cigarette had an unpleasant taste: it stung and scratched his throat, which was already dry from the strong, harsh wind. But the taste was not completely unfamiliar. He strained to remember when he'd experienced it before. It was the taste of his very first cigarette, to which his father had treated him. They had been bouncing along in a rickety wagon; the wind was blowing in their faces; the cigarette stung his throat, choking him. He could still see himself flicking the cigarette onto the dusty road, and he repeated the same gesture now.

The truck pulled off the road and stopped beside the edge of a fragrant forest. It was midafternoon. The men pulled sausage links out of their bundles. The smell of garlic overpowered the aroma of the pine needles.

And now how dramatically the kernel of euphoria swelled at the sight of all those trees shadowing the dappled forest floor! Jozef scrambled down from the truck and rushed into the forest. The girl's haste was harder to explain, but she, too, jumped down, running after Jozef. They both disappeared into the green depths, between the bright splashes of sunlight and the luxurious ferns. When the girl caught up with him, Jozef was already lying under a tree, stretched out on the velvety moss, breathing deeply. A tranquil smile played on his face.

Breathless from running, the girl spoke first. She said she couldn't remain alone in the truck with those drunks. She was afraid they would start telling their murder stories all over again. That's why she ran after him. She said she was at the end of her rope, especially since yesterday—

Her voice broke, and Jozef, who had been listening in silence, gently interrupted. "Don't. Please. Not now . . ."

The girl frowned and said sarcastically, "You act like you're on some sort of spring picnic!"

"As a matter of fact," Jozef replied, "this is a perfect spot for a spring picnic," and he noticed how a tiny accordion of wrinkles furrowed the girl's brow—the same wrinkles that had appeared when he whistled the aria from *Rigoletto*. Averting his eyes, he added, "Just take a look around and you'll see that I'm right. Of course it's already autumn. So it would be better to call it an autumn picnic. Let's enjoy our autumn picnic!"

The girl, who didn't know him and was certainly unaware of the kernel of euphoria, muttered one word that made it very clear what she thought about Jozef and his lying there on the moss. He heard her. And what of it? He let it go, let it vanish into the forest, and went on:

"Yes, that's right, let's enjoy our autumn picnic. Do as I do. Sit down on the moss and appreciate the rare beauty of ordinary things: the singing of the birds, the sound of the wind in the trees, the smell of the pine needles. . . ."

Undeterred by her silence, ignoring the deepening accordion folds, he declared that he had never in his life sufficiently appreciated the beauty of perfect picnic spots like this one, and that he deeply regretted that now. Furthermore, he felt that this was the source of the strength that—

"Please stop babbling! For God's sake, stop!" the girl screamed, and covered her ears with her hands.

Jozef fell silent. But it was the wrong moment for silence. A drunken song about recent events wafted over from the truck. Jozef scraped up some moss with his fingers, brought the little green cushion up to his eyes, and examined it closely. Perhaps he would have been able to find shelter in the safe green softness were it not for the next sound he heard, a sound he at first mistook for the chirping of a bird. The girl was crying with her face buried in her hands. Her whole body was rocking back and forth, like that of an old woman consumed by grief.

He flung down the moss and stretched out his hand. He was not accustomed to displays of tenderness. He did what he had often done to his landlady's cat, in secret: he ran his palm along the girl's firm, curly hair. "It's all right, kitty, it's all right," he used to say. And now he said, "Don't cry . . . it's all right . . . don't cry . . ."

She cried out, "You don't know what they . . . yesterday, they—" But he didn't let her finish this time either.

"I know," he said tenderly, "I know. I know everything."

At last, she stopped crying and, like a child, came for comfort. She put her head on his chest, and snuggled close, in despair. And they lay there entwined in the green depths of the woods, between the bright splashes of sunlight and the luxuriant ferns, and his hand caressed the roiling black sea of her hair.

He felt a painful but not unpleasant pressure in his heart, the symptom of a chemical change in the nature of the kernel. Whereas it had been as light as a soap bubble, now it must have sustained some harm, some small wound, through which a thick, painful poison was seeping, like water into a leaking boat.

When they returned to the truck they took the same seats they had before, far apart. Jozef was relieved by the distance, after their closeness in the forest. He sat facing forward, intent on his own thoughts. He felt the oppressive weight of the pebble pressing against his heart. That was what had become of the kernel of euphoria, light as a soap bubble. Mortally wounded, brimming with painful poison, it had turned to stone. But even in its present form it retained its peculiar ways; in defiance of natural law, the pebble was growing and expanding so that it was soon transformed from a pebble into a stone, which weighed more and more heavily on Jozef's breast.

They were descending into the broad river valley. The end of the journey was approaching, and as often happens near the end of a trip, the travelers were overcome by exhaustion. The men fell into a sodden sleep, and the only sound was the clinking of empty vodka bottles.

An iron bridge rumbled under the wheels of the truck. Jozef woke from his daze, looked around and listened.

He heard the rattle of a wagon coming toward them. The driver was waving his whip: behind him, on a seat covered with straw, sat a man in a dark suit and a stiff hat and, beside him, a young boy. When they came close, Jozef suddenly caught sight of a large onion-shaped watch and heard the faint click of its cover. The hour hand glided around the white face.

"Are we going to be late, Papa?" He heard his own voice.

And his father's voice: "What do you mean, 'late'? Don't worry. You have your whole life ahead of you. . . ."

The pain was so intense that Jozef pressed his hand to his

heart. His whole life ahead of him! He gasped—or maybe it was a groan. His whole life . . . he saw his father's eyes full of trust and hope. And what has come of it? he asked himself, and answered his own question: Nothing . . . nothing . . .

A dark cylinder appeared on the horizon. At first he was puzzled, but after a while he recognized the smokestack of the brick works located far outside town. But still he was amazed. He looked at the landscape of his childhood as he might have looked at an old friend whom he hadn't seen in years and who had changed beyond recognition. They were driving through the flat monotonous plains of the steppe. Narrow footpaths wound through the fields, and white statues of saints stood at the crossroads. Everything smelled of heather and thyme. And when the town finally appeared in the valley, at the foot of Castle Hill, it, too, amazed him with its changed appearance. The church tower had vanished into the background, behind the roofs of the town. The river and Castle Hill seemed to have switched places. Then he understood. He was returning along a road he had traveled only once before, when his father had driven him to the railroad station in a rickety wagon. He had been going away to the big city to study.

That was the only time he had driven on this road. Beginning with his first vacation, he'd come home by train, on the new railroad line, which had been built that same year. From the windows of the train the little town welcomed travelers with its church tower, and the woods they called the Black Forest came up almost as far as the station.

The smokestack of the brick works and the steppe were invisible.

This discovery moved Jozef deeply. The words "first," "last," "fate," "destiny," rattled around in his weary brain. He did not try to resist. Something had been completed once and for all, some sort of circle had been closed. As he was formulating this difficult idea, he thought those exact words: "something" and "some sort of." He was afraid of bigger words, grander words, although now more than ever they would have been appropriate.

The first houses at the edge of town appeared. The truck pulled over to the side of the road and stopped. The driver turned off the engine. No one knows what woke the men: the sudden silence or the girl's long, drawn-out scream of terror.

A procession of people was moving along the road that led through the outskirts of town. They were guarded by men in uniforms who were holding rifles, ready to shoot. Deaf to the girl's cry and to the men's excited voices, Jozef pressed against the side rails of the truck and observed his own fate attentively, and with intense concentration.

The thoughtfulness of the driver, who had pulled off the road and stopped his truck, turned out to be unnecessary. The uniformed men diverted the procession onto the track that wound through the flat steppe. Only the last figure in the procession, a figure in helmet and uniform, paused for a moment, thinking. Then he headed toward the truck that was parked by the side of the road.

A SECOND SCRAP OF TIME

A vast distance separated the old time from the new, the space between the first SS operation—which we still called a roundup—and the second, which for the first time we called by its proper name, *Aktion*. This new time did not displace the old time all at once; we had grown accustomed to the old time, we felt at home in it—so that the process occurred slowly, almost imperceptibly. But the change was nevertheless inevitable, and by the end of the second *Aktion* (which was the first to be called that), the new time was firmly established. This second *Aktion* had certain qualities that defined it more precisely.

The space separating both operations was a borderland. Pushed to the limits of the old time, we slowly inched our way into the new zone, our progress constantly thwarted by false hopes and inaccurate calculations, until finally we found ourselves fully under the new time's power. We had no idea how it happened: everything was planned so cunningly that at first none of us realized we were under siege.

In assessing the situation we unwittingly resorted to

oversimplification; we viewed our slow crawl into the new zone as a series of separate "troubles." What we failed to realize was that by dividing this movement into doses and degrees we were growing accustomed to it. By using everyday language to describe it, we were creating whole new categories of thought and learning new responses that, in the old time, would surely have been considered insane.

In our daily lives we clung to familiar habits and routines—undressing for bed and eating meals together at the table—and just added new ones. The simplest example: Instead of greeting one another with the usual small talk—How are you? What's new? It's warm out today—we used new phrases, "There was an *Aktion* in T.," "Are things quiet in town?" or "I heard they killed two boys at Reckmann's camp." After that we'd serve our guests tea (brewed from the petals of a garden rose) or cigarettes (rolled from shag tobacco), or else the barley meal that we lived on at that time.

Our vocabulary sprouted new expressions and strange acronyms for long names, but the word *Aktion* towered above them all. It dominated that time that some people—in their misguided naïveté—continued to call wartime.

The space between the first *Aktion* and the second was vast. The leaves fell from the trees, the snow covered the ground, and the ice broke up on the river that flowed lazily through the city, with a branch running beside the public bath. The night of the second *Aktion* was the first time—but not the last time—that this bathhouse was converted into a warehouse, where the human harvest was stored for transport.

That was the night the ice broke up, with its loud hissing and cracking. The powerful voice of the river rumbling through the garden muffled the footsteps of the man who suddenly appeared at our door, panting and trembling. Before he could say a word, we knew that it had begun; we were clever students of the new time. The panting, trembling man sank back into the darkness to reappear—like a messenger crying "Fire!"—at another house, another threshold under the Star of David.

We still didn't know that this *Aktion* was special, different, set apart from the one that came before and those that came after. All of us, young and old alike, uttered a few brief, helpless cries as we rushed out of the house and toward the river's roaring, into the thick darkness, entrusting our lives to a few bare bushes in the garden.

One by one we ran down the puddle-soaked path, toward the hiss of steaming water and the shattering of ice, until someone shouted—and stopped us in our tracks. Someone was calling us to come back. Who? What words did he use, how did he tell us that we were not in danger, because we were young and healthy—both in body and in mind? I don't know.

Everything is dark—nothing, a void—until the moment I find myself sitting on the bench beside the kitchen window, clutching a piece of coarse bread. A sputtering candle, a woman's cry, fingers digging into an arm.

The *Aktion* of the old, the sick, and the crippled.

The relief must have been great, that is, relief as defined by the standards of the new time: a death sentence had suddenly been commuted. I don't remember the relief, but my sitting in the kitchen seems like irrefutable testimony that it existed—my clutching the bread, the way I tore at it without eating it, the thin candle with its sputtering flame dispersing the darkness.

Then there was a different kind of light, a weak flash lasting no more than one or two seconds—just long enough for me to see fingers digging into an arm wrapped in rough homespun, and a woman's face. The flash was preceded by a strange birdlike whistle, equally weak, and shrill, which seemed to be coming down the street, and the closer it came the more birdlike and less human it sounded. I moved closer to the window and pressed my face against the windowpane, hoping to see an owl or some other night bird. I was sweating.

With the whistle came steps, running, first far away, then closer and closer. The running was uneven, intermittent, as if the runner, having built up speed, were forced to stop, suddenly, and then forced to race on. And all the time the odd noise, which, now that my ears had grown used to it, no longer seemed birdlike at all. Now I could tell that it was a human cry, wretched and despairing.

It would have passed by nameless in the night if it hadn't been for a thin sword of light that cut white through the darkness. The search beam vanished as suddenly as it had appeared—but still I managed to see.

In a fraction of a second I saw an arm wrapped in rough homespun. I saw fingers, fierce and clawing, pressed into the arm. And in the same split second, I saw the old, worn face of Perla the fisherwoman, known throughout town as the crazy woman who used whatever money she scrounged from begging to buy fish, which she then tossed into the pond. No one had ever heard her voice: she herself was as quiet as a fish. But now she was crying out. She was screaming that she didn't want to be dragged off to be executed. She pronounced the word "executed" carefully, one syllable at a time, with perfect diction. At the last moment her mind had come back to her, along with her speech.

When the cries ceased and everything grew quiet once again, I sat back down on the bench and began to nibble on the coarse bread. Soon I had eaten our family's entire ration for the next several days.

Outside the window the spruces and the jagged line of the picket fence began to take shape. I walked onto the porch, opened the door, and stood on the threshold. The air was fresh and humid. The noise of the river had grown softer; the water level must have fallen during the night. A pale dawn gleamed over the town. The crowing of the roosters broke the silence, and soon after, three figures appeared at the far end of the street. Two young women were leading a third, who was gray haired and trembling. "It's over, Mama," I heard one of the young ones saying. "Don't be afraid. You're alive, Mama." The second one turned to me and said, "We hid Mama in the potato cellar."

The first reports leaked out the next morning. They came from Polish railwaymen, who talked about a train made of freight cars bleached with slaked lime and bound for a place called Belzec. We had never heard of it. The name called to mind the popular song that began "Belz, my little town, Belz," but it turned out to be a different place entirely.

IN FRONT OF THE MIRROR

One gloomy December afternoon Adela decided to shorten her dress, so she put on her father's shoes and ran over to her friend Nisia the dressmaker's. Nisia had been living nearby for a year; in those days, everybody lived nearby. By the time Adela burst into the little room on the ground floor, she was completely out of breath. Nisia was sitting next to the window, which overlooked the bare stone courtyard. A clean dish towel was draped across her knees; on top of the dish towel sat a frying pan. Nisia was eating her dinner of leftover potatoes. A large, heavy shovel was propped against the windowsill. Nisia's hands were rough and cracked; there was no sewing machine in the room. Nisia had sold it; she hadn't done any sewing for a long time. Now all she needed was a shovel, for constructing a big bridge across a small river—just like Adela, in fact, who also had a shovel at home, for loading coal at the railroad station.

Adela closed the door behind her, stamped the snow off her shoes, and sat down on a stool that had once belonged to Nisia's father, a shoemaker. Nisia did not interrupt her dinner; with slow, measured movements she scraped the potatoes from the pan and chewed them with difficulty.

There were four beds in the room; three of them were no longer needed. The first one had been vacated over the summer, the next in early autumn, and the third a little time later. The fourth was for Nisia, who, without interrupting her dinner, listened to Adela chattering away as she sat there on her father's stool.

After she finished eating her potatoes, she stood up. She was delicate and still pretty, even though the three beds had been vacated one after the other, and the fourth would soon be free. She rinsed the pan in cold water and hung it on a hook above the kitchen stove, which had grown cold long ago and never been relit. She warmed her potatoes on a little iron ring.

"You say you want it shortened?" she said, and Adela eagerly nodded her head.

"It needs to be shortened and taken in at the hips, because I've lost weight."

They went over to the big mirror, which shone in the depths of the room like a rippling, murky yellow lake.

"Right here, you see . . . ," Adela whispered, "that's where it bunches up."

Nisia took up the material with a practiced gesture, just a little too rough and too abrupt for a dressmaker. Their eyes met at the bottom of the murky lake, Nisia's with just a hint of a sneer.

"Do you know, Adela, that there's nobody left in the

whole building but me?" she said to the other pair of eyes, which glittered huge and feverish.

"Just do what needs doing, Nisia. Don't talk. I'm not listening to what you're saying." And Adela put her hands over her ears.

But Nisia insisted. "Did you hear? Nobody but me—"

"Just do what needs doing." The other girl cut her off.

So Nisia knelt down beside the girl pretending to be deaf, reached for the bristling pincushion that she still kept from her former tailoring days, and, picking out one rusty pin, looked up at the face looming out of the yellow depths. Adela's face was radiant.

"Adela, how can you? Aren't you ashamed . . . ? Adela . . ."

"Don't be so stupid!" Adela burst out laughing and brought her glowing face close to the surface of the mirror, as if she wanted to get a better look at herself. "This is my first love. My first and only." She smiled at her own face.

At the sight of Adela's full, moist lips, parted in a smile, Nisia felt a sudden pang and shut her eyes.

"Don't be so stupid," Adela continued. "Don't you think I understand? There are empty beds in my house, too. I know everything there is to know. And I wish I didn't."

She bent over the girl kneeling at her feet, and then added, gently, with the unruffled conviction of the self-righteous, "Just do what needs doing, Nisia, and don't worry about it."

"Tell me," the kneeling girl whispered. "Tell me, is it possible . . . that you're happy?"

The light in Adela's eyes and the radiance of her face confirmed this incomprehensible and cruel possibility. Horrified, Nisia the dressmaker began to sob.

After she calmed down, she shortened Adela's dress with quick, adept movements of her hands, which had grown thick and clumsy from the shovel; and then, to check her work, she raised her eyes to the mirror.

Night had fallen over the murky yellow lake, turning the water black. Adela and her happiness were swallowed by the dark abyss.

THE DEATH OF TSARITSA

The death of Tsaritsa would have remained one of a million anonymous deaths were it not for the fact that it happened on a beautiful, mild day. (I've only imagined that the day was mild; much of what I'm going to say—but only the details, not the event itself—is the product of my imagination.) It happened in the very early evening, when the trees cast long shadows and the air was saturated with a light blue haze that was growing deeper and darker by the minute, although it was still long before nightfall. Tsaritsa's death happened at just the hour best suited for strolling, the hour that lures people onto the streets after a hard day's work.

B., too, decided to go for a walk through the streets that already lay under the long shadows of the setting sun, and it was this decision that rescued Tsaritsa's death from anonymity, that summoned a witness who could then place the death precisely in time and space. When B. crouched down beside her, Tsaritsa was still alive. But soon after, she stopped breathing.

She didn't look at all like a tsaritsa. She was more like a comely village girl, with a ruddy, round face and dimpled cheeks. Her hair was coarse and thick. She laughed a lot, showing her very small, very white teeth. Her laugh was high and playful, but she herself was dignified and stately. When we called her Tsaritsa, we were taking our cue from a certain poet. He was drinking raw eggs one winter's day when Stefania entered the room; she was covered with snow, all rosy from the cold, wearing a black sheepskin cap and high boots. The poet put the egg down on the window-sill and cried out, "Tsaritsa!" He was skinny and sported a small, pointed beard; next to Tsaritsa he looked like a little elf. So "Tsaritsa" she remained, since the poets' power is great over us even when they see a crown and a throne where we see a haystack. She was delighted by her new name; she burst out laughing, pleased and playful, and that was probably how she laughed when she saw Kürch coming toward her down the street. Surprised and amazed, Kürch (I imagine) cried out "Stefania!" when he saw her. He called her Stefania, in the Polish way, not Steffi: further evidence of his kindness.

The other gendarmes (she worked as a cleaning woman for the Feldgendarmerie) called her Steffi.

I don't know which street it was, probably one of the major streets, very likely the main street itself, an avenue bordered by a double row of trees that arched over the road between them. The street ended in a round plaza with a fountain, gleaming towers, and cupolas. That's where I imagine the meeting between Stefania and Kürch, the sickly

German with the bald, pear-shaped head, wearing his round eyeglasses and dressed, of course, in the uniform of the Feldgendarmerie. Moreover, it seems to me that it had to take place precisely near that plaza with its fountain, surrounded by benches and jasmine bushes, since that is where the mothers usually sat with their children, and no doubt Stefania was there with that child. I don't know if the child was a boy or a girl, but I do know what Kürch looked like because I saw him once.

I saw him once in the peasant cottage where Stefania and her parents were living after they had been forced out of their house. It was on the outskirts of the little town (Stefania's hometown and mine) in a garden, and it was so low that the mallows and other red flowers reached the windows. It was a picturesque hut filled with the smell of wild herbs and mint. Only now do I note its picturesqueness; at the time I thought, It's well situated, so close to the forest.

Stefania's mother, a tiny woman, had just lit the oil lamp (there was no electricity in the hut), and we were drinking tea brewed from the petals of the roses that flowered in the garden. The tea was fragrant, though weak. The sky was growing dark, and we heard footsteps out in the yard. Mother and daughter exchanged knowing glances, both said *"Bitte"* out loud, and Kürch entered the room. His glasses glinted in the light from the oil lamp; he did not say *"Heil Hitler,"* just *"Guten Abend,"* in the accent of a Saxon peasant. I assume that he felt at home in that cottage; perhaps it reminded him of his home in Saxony. Stefania should have realized that, and later on, she should have remembered it.

Kürch placed a bottle of wine on the table, discreetly, a little embarrassed, and smiled. "So . . . well . . . how are things?"

He slurped his tea, and his nose turned red. He didn't stay long, maybe because I was there, gaping wordlessly at him. He mentioned a letter from home. He didn't show any photographs, maybe because he'd shown them on another occasion.

He got to his feet reluctantly and said a lengthy goodbye. Stefania smiled indulgently, playfully.

"A decent man," she said as we stood by the window and watched him walking down the road toward town. "He's ashamed of all this; he sympathizes with us. It bothers him that I have to wash floors for them. He visits us often, and it's thanks to him that I'm still working there and have legitimate papers—a good *Ausweis.*"

What did her parents say to Kürch when their daughter suddenly disappeared? I assume that no such conversation took place. Stefania disappeared from our little town the day before everyone had to move into the ghetto. She was the first who dared take such a step. Where did she go? How? No one knew; no one asked.

Only after the war B.—not Stefania's parents, who were killed—told us that she had worked as a nanny for a German family in a city some two hundred kilometers away. He had lived in the same part of town and had seen her often, usually by chance; she spent a lot of time in the fresh air, in the parks and squares.

So when she saw a sickly man with a pear-shaped head coming toward her along that street that I keep imagining, she did not hesitate for a moment: perhaps she even quickened her pace. I know she did not hesitate, because even if she couldn't have avoided that meeting (which, although she did not know it, would decide her fate), she wasn't obliged to speak. But she did. A picture emerged from the darkness of that other world, by then as distant as another planet: the peasant cottage, Kürch sitting at her parents' table, slurping tea or drinking wine. Kürch in the uniform of the Feldgendarmerie was not just Kürch; he was a cloud of memories swirling around her—her home, her parents, her native town, her mother's voice, and undoubtedly his voice, too, Kürch's voice, sympathizing with them, grieving over their fate. I know that she did not hesitate, and that he blurted out her name, surprised to recognize in the smiling girl the same Stefania he'd undoubtedly long presumed dead, exterminated, surprised to see her leading a plump child by the hand and not wearing a white armband. I know he blurted out her name (it had to have been that way). What I don't know is exactly when—was it when she held out her hand to him with a confident smile, or later, when she told him what had happened?—his surprise gave way to amazement at how the order of things had fallen apart, and he filled in the details.

She ought to have expected it, she ought to have feared it, but she didn't expect it, and she didn't fear it. It's astonishing how untouched she was by the time, how alien to her were its laws and its sacred regulations. She had kept her sense of trust intact, and in those days trust stemmed from a lack of imagination. I suppose that she even told her employer about the meeting and let her know that she was expecting a visitor.

B. said he went out for a stroll around town before dark, so her death must have occurred, as I mentioned, in the early evening, when the sun was setting and a thin haze blanketed the town and the shadows of trees lay on the streets.

Although I can see her meeting on the street with Kürch quite clearly, I have never been able to imagine the way they rushed in, the words they spoke, the expression on Tsaritsa's face (now she has again become Tsaritsa for me), the flash of terror at the moment she realized what was happening.

Only the jump itself, that hurtling of the body—there were three of them, Kürch and two others, they were standing in the middle of the big room with its window open over the trees on the quiet street, five floors up—only the jump itself, the hurtling of the body and her flight toward the earth and the sudden upward rush of sky, the flight that tore her from the laws of that time and returned her to the everlasting law of gravity, which applies equally to everyone. Now, imagining the moment of her death, I begin to fully appreciate the poet's exclamation.

Walking along the quiet street, B. heard shouts; he saw a small crowd gathered around three Germans in uniform.

He instinctively pushed the people aside and bent over the woman on the ground. Tsaritsa was still alive. Her eyes were open, fixed on the sky, which during her flight had rushed upward and stayed there, suspended, the moment her body touched the earth.

EUGENIA

The promenade atop Castle Hill, flat as a table. Above the path, a nest of green branches; beneath the trees, benches, empty in the noonday sun. The promenade itself, where the entire town liked to stroll, was also empty—except for the two of us, Eugenia and I. My parents had already disappeared behind the gate into the park, leaving only the two of us perched on the high promenade, with the whole town stretched out at our feet, the houses and gardens, the sleepy river, and the still, gray pond, everything dead calm in the heat of that July afternoon.

I'm sure it was July, because my mother noted the date on the back of a photo taken two hours later: "15 July 37."

It was the same day when, on our way to Pani Malvina's, Mother's kindly friend who had invited us to tea, Eugenia made her peculiar declaration. Just like that, out of the blue, she proclaimed that she wished to die in an automobile accident, on some beautiful, sunny day, along a twisting mountain road, intoxicated by the beauty of life and nature. A car plunging into the brink, one split second, and that would be that. I looked at her in amazement. I was thirteen years old; she was almost forty, and all our conversations generally revolved around ordinary, everyday matters such as school, books, girlfriends.

Not that there were so many occasions for conversation, since Eugenia lived far from us, in Silesia, a stone's throw away from the Germans, whereas we lived in the east, a stone's throw away from the Russians. She came once a year, to spend her vacation with my mother, her oldest sister. She slept in the dining room, on a narrow sofa bed, which suited her, since she was petite and fragile as a consequence, we were told, of the hunger years during the First World War. Another consequence of those years was her crippled little finger, which an operation had made twice as small as it had been, so that it curled from her right hand, almost comical, always pink, meticulously manicured.

Eugenia was nothing if not meticulous—with her appearance, with her housework, and undoubtedly with her shorthand as well. She worked in a smoggy Germanized town (a stone's throw away from the Germans) as a secretary to a director of a coal firm, taking shorthand and typing business letters in three languages. Later, and on more than one occasion, I attributed her excessively precise approach to those German surroundings.

Her face was round, with fine, delicate features. She wore tiny, elegant shoes. Every evening she shut her balcony door and latched it tight; she was afraid the frogs might hop in from the garden.

On that July day, I looked at her in amazement, surprised by her unexpected confession, her wish to die a violent death in a beautiful landscape. I was surprised and concerned. I wanted to say something, to ask her where she got such ideas, but she didn't wait for me to say anything; she acted as if she hadn't been speaking to me at all and walked off briskly on her thin legs. The dress she wore that day was the color of ripe cherries; years later she gave that dress to me, and I was wearing it the day they took me to the forced labor camp.

No sooner do I write "forced labor camp" (actually it writes itself) than the promenade atop Castle Hill disappears and is replaced by potato fields, a gray autumn fog, and the shouts of Ukrainian guards . . . for just a few seconds, though, because now we're both emerging from the fog: Eugenia is walking faster, not looking at me, but at the still, faraway pond; on her head she's wearing a hat tilted at a coquettish angle and resembling a bird's nest.

A car plunging into the brink, one split second . . . why? I wondered, but I didn't ask. Now I know how smart her wish really was.

We had just passed the gate to the park and spotted the house inside the grounds that belonged to Pani Malvina and her mustachioed husband. We saw the table on the porch, set for tea; in front of the porch my parents were greeting the hosts and their son, a handsome man, no longer young. It was he who photographed us later on the lawn beneath the pine trees, using a camera equipped with a self-timer, so that he, too, appears in the picture. He's standing with a cigarette in his hand and watching

Eugenia—closely, fondly—from the corner of his eye. She's turned her head away, gazing off to the side. It wasn't until after the war, when I was looking at the picture, which just by chance happened to survive, that I noticed his fond gaze and her turned head and thought that maybe my mother's friend, with her unmarried son, no longer young, and my mother herself, with her unmarried sister, no longer young, had some intention, some hope, some quiet design.

Two days after the tea, Eugenia left unexpectedly. Her departure was preceded by a long-distance phone call, equally unexpected, since no one ever telephoned for her. She spoke very briefly over the phone, then announced she had to leave the following day. Mother looked at her without a word. The next morning we took the buggy to the station. That summer was dry; the trees lining the road were dusty. The buggy traveled straight to the crossroads outside town and took a right turn, toward the station.

We still had five years left, we and Eugenia. Five years later she would be the only one of us to take the same road the buggy was taking now, except she would turn left at the crossroads, into the fields. No mountains, no twisting curves, only the flat steppe. But we still had another five years ahead of us.

The train arrived empty; it was on its way back from the station at the border. Eugenia stood framed in the window—small and lonely amid the empty compartments. She waved good-bye, her little finger curling from her hand.

That evening, when it was time to water the flower beds, our neighbor Paulina asked my mother, "Why doesn't your Genia get married? She's so pretty, educated, with a good job . . . ?"

"Evidently she hasn't met anybody she wants to marry."

Paulina said, "Time's flying, and she's not getting any younger."

"Are your roses covered with aphids, too?" answered my mother. "It's a real plague."

Eugenia left in the summer and came back in the winter. It was 1938. She came back in the winter, although she was dreadfully afraid of the cold; where we lived, a stone's throw away from the Russians, the mercury in the thermometer was sinking dramatically. She didn't like the snow either, which was piling up in front of the house in huge drifts. But she came back nevertheless.

It was 1938, Hitler's fifth year in Berlin, and we could already hear rumblings of what was to come, though only rumblings. The Brownshirts issued various interdictions and injunctions but it should be noted that a certain German, a doctor in Silesia, refused to comply. I didn't find out about this doctor until after the war, when Julia, my mother's other sister, mentioned him to me. She described him as elderly, balding, with a kind face and thoughtful eyes, although she knew him only from a picture; neither she nor anyone else in the family had ever met him. At any rate, for several years this certain German, whose friendship with Eugenia was shrouded in secrecy and silence, refused to comply. But that frosty winter during Hitler's fifth year in Berlin he suddenly came around, completely, unexpectedly. Unexpectedly for Eugenia, that is, since he had surely been considering this step for a while.

Julia told me about him in a beautiful, rambling park that had survived the war unspoiled, in a ruined city that had until recently been German, so naturally it reminded me of our park on Castle Hill, and the sentence Eugenia had spoken along the promenade came back word for word. It was then I figured out that the kind German with thoughtful eyes, who finally came around during Hitler's fifth year in power, must have abandoned Eugenia that winter she came to visit.

Leave Genia alone, Mother had told us. She has to rest, she's overworked, she needs some peace and quiet. Agafia glared angrily and muttered something under her breath, but nonetheless obediently stoked the stoves twice a day. And still Eugenia seemed cold. She went to bed early, her sofa bed guarded by the woolen slippers she placed on the floor, with meticulous neatness, side by side. They were from Zakopane, embroidered with thistles. I remember them well. And I remember Eugenia's face, which seemed smaller than it had been, more haggard.

"And what about the kind German?" I asked Julia.

"He left for Germany. That's all she said and never said another word about it."

"They couldn't have drafted him into the Wehrmacht. He was too old for that. But who knows? Maybe he went on to be a doctor in some camp."

Julia replied that she didn't like to speculate; it was hard enough coping with what she already knew for a fact. "He stole the best years of her life; it took Eugenia a long time to recover her footing. And by then it was too late."

The unspoiled park in the ruined city had many large clearings and shady paths interrupted by murmuring brooks. I stopped speaking, and so did Julia. The acorns crackled under our feet as we strolled under the trees in silence, each engrossed in her own thoughts.

"Intoxicated by the beauty of life and nature." Only now does the pathos of those words strike me; only now do I understand.

A year later and the Germans were a stone's throw away from us, along the River Bug, only a short distance from our own little Gniezna. Eugenia fled Silesia and came to stay with us for good.

When I write "for good," I mean that she had no intention of going anywhere, that she planned to remain with us until the end of the war. Only later did those words acquire a different meaning. At the time no one knew how long the war would last: some predicted it would drag on, others claimed it would soon be over, but no one had the faintest inkling of what was really in store.

This time Eugenia looked even smaller. She seemed to have shrunk and grown quieter. She had long talks with Mother and seldom left the house. In the morning she would wrap a scarf tightly around her head, to protect her hair, and meticulously and systematically dust the books in the library. She bemoaned (very quietly) the fact that Dostoyevsky was dusty, or that Heine was dog-eared. Agafia was angry at her for not minding her own business. In the evening Eugenia would sit by the radio, turning the knob; whenever the speakers burst into a torrent of barking German, she would put her hands to her temples as if struck by a sudden headache.

Our neighbor Paulina, on the other hand, kept going on mindlessly about the same thing—Your sister keeps to herself, doesn't she? The pharmacist's son has his eye on her; you ought to have a talk with her. Mother said nothing: perhaps her silence meant that she agreed with Paulina; it's impossible to tell.

The Germans were a stone's throw away from us, and the Russians were already there.

Our house shrank: two rooms were commandeered to billet the officers. There were three of them; the oldest and highest ranking, a lover of Bach, warned us to watch out for the middle one, since he was a *politruk*—a Party official assigned to the military. The youngest, on the other hand, handsome in a rakish sort of way, had no sooner arrived than he asked Agafia to take him to the Orthodox church, preferably when it was evening and nearly dark.

The oldest and highest ranking would soon save Eugenia from being deported to Siberia, although by saving her then he was unwittingly condemning her to death later. And she, happy, thanked him for pulling her off the transport, which traveled for three weeks before stopping somewhere in the northern taiga.

Have I said "happy"? I was wrong. I never saw her really happy, not even when she was laughing. Maybe only once, and then she frightened me, since that was in the ghetto, in the last months of its existence, near the very end.

That was when she stepped into the room and stood by the door, looking at all of us, at Father (Mother was already dead), at Julia and her husband, at my sister and me, and we looked at her standing there, smiling impishly, as if she'd just pulled some prank. We stared in amazement at her metamorphosis, because it wasn't Eugenia standing in the doorway, it was someone else, years younger, with a bright face, and—it's hard to find any other word—happy.

She had cut her hair; normally tied up in back, it was now trimmed short in an even fringe around her head.

That was the day my sister and I escaped from the ghetto; it was the last time I saw Eugenia.

Julia emerged from her reverie and repeated: "By then it was too late." She asked whether I remembered Emanuel, who had escaped from Lodz and wound up staying in the ghetto. Because when she said "it was too late," she was thinking of him.

Then she said one more sentence (which she didn't finish) about sudden love in the dying ghetto, powerful and tender, torn from life, the love that Eugenia . . .

I didn't ask any more questions.

Eugenia and Emanuel died in the last *Aktion*, when the ghetto was liquidated. One more week, and they were supposed to join Julia and her husband hiding in the miller's attic. But where Eugenia and Emanuel were living, there was nowhere to hide.

Just after the war, Olga the seamstress came over and said that from the window of her house, which overlooked the road to the station, she had witnessed the last procession from the ghetto.

She had seen Eugenia walking along the side of the road; a tall man with a slight stoop had his arm around her. They passed right beneath her window.

DESCRIPTION OF A MORNING

A young WOMAN *is sitting on a straw mattress. A young* MAN *stands in front of her. He is exercising: arms up, arms out, inhale, exhale. They are in an attic, or really a part of an attic. The roof is slanted: the walls are made of wooden planks.*

MAN: Klara, please. I'm waiting. After all, you promised, you said I was right. Klara, please. *(Pause.)* Well since you don't want to . . . *(Goes on exercising.)*

(The WOMAN *sits with her eyes closed, motionless.)*

MAN: That's enough for today. *(He hesitates a moment, then walks over to the wooden wall, puts his eye to a crack, and peers outside.)* It's getting light out. The farmyard's still empty. I'll wait for the hens. I've come to like those hens. They're so cheerful. Always chattering away. Especially the spotted one. But the crested one is nice, too. That's right. Nice. I know every single hen. They're not all alike you know: there are hens and there are hens. *(He puts his other eye to the crack.)* They're still asleep. Maybe it's Sunday. I've lost track. I told you we should have gone on with our calendar. *(Pause.)* There's the farmer wife. She's coming out of the house, she's carrying a bucket. So it's not Sunday, on Sundays she does the milking later. But she has her Sunday scarf on, the red one. And a clean apron. She's standing on the threshold. She's blowing her nose; she's wiping her hands on her apron. She's put down the bucket to sweep the yard. Want to take a look? . . . She isn't very thorough: she missed a pile of manure over in the right-hand corner. She's in a hurry. Now she's gone to the hen-house. Klara, we're so lucky to have this crack. *(He watches in silence.)* Oh, she's let them out. There's the snow-white one, the crested one's right behind. One, two, three, four, five, six, seven. There's one missing. Maybe they butchered it, who knows . . . I like hens. They've run off. . . . You won't be able to see them. Too bad. *(He wipes his eyes.)* It's tiring, switching eyes like that. And now let's have some breakfast. *(He hands the* WOMAN *a piece of bread and a cup of water.)* Eat. You have to eat. The bread's stale, but thank God for it anyway.

(Reflexively, the WOMAN *lifts her hand to her mouth, then drops it. She opens her eyes.)*

MAN: Go ahead. Eat.

WOMAN: What were you saying during the night?

MAN: I couldn't sleep.

WOMAN: What were you saying?

MAN: I was trying to remember all the last names of my fifth-grade pupils. In alphabetical order. There are so many names I've already forgotten. I stopped at *S*.

WOMAN: At *S*.

MAN: At *S*. Maybe you remember the name of that little freckled boy who used to come see us every now and then.

WOMAN: Süss.

MAN: That's it. Süss. Tyczynski, Wesolowski, Zylberstein.

WOMAN: I saw them take Süss away.

MAN: Klara . . . you promised. . . .

WOMAN: All right.

MAN: Süss, Tyczynski, Wesolowski. Oh no, first Winkler, and then Zylberstein.

WOMAN: Could you please stop talking for just a moment?

MAN: Of course—if it bothers you so much. *(He looks through the crack.)* Not a hen in sight. The bucket's right in front of the stable. The yard is empty. A pile of manure in the right-hand corner . . . The farmer's wife has left the stable. She's blowing her nose. She's taken off her scarf to scratch her head. She's picked up the bucket and is heading for the house. The yard is empty. There's nothing to see. *(He sits back down on the straw mattress.)* What's the plan for today?

(The WOMAN *covers her ears with her hands.)*

MAN: Gymnastics, breakfast, Latin grammar, the next installment of our spoken novel. You've covered your ears. But you admitted I was right, Klara, you agreed it was necessary. It's our only protection.

(The WOMAN *lies down on the mattress, still covering her ears.)*

MAN: I'll ask the farmer again. Maybe he'll look around for a book. If we sat next to the crack we'd have enough light to read by.

WOMAN: He won't bring any books. He'd be afraid. Why would he need a book? What's he going to say when they ask whom it's for?

(A shot is heard.)

MAN: *(Jumping up and putting his eye to the crack.)* Somebody fired a gun. Who? Where? At whom? The farmer's run out of the house. He's buttoning his pants. It must be Sunday after all, he's wearing his woolen trousers. Or maybe it's some kind of holiday. . . . His dog's run after him. He's up by the gate looking toward the village. He's standing there looking. *(Pause.)* He's coming back. He's yawning. He's fixing his pants. Now he's bending over and petting Burek. He's calm. The shot didn't bother him. He's going back inside; he's closed the door. The yard is empty. . . . So, where were we? Chapter three. Mrs. Brown returns to her uncle. She still doesn't know about the theft. She arrived with the night train. It's early in the morning. Let's begin with the description of the morning. Descriptions of nature can be very soothing. Klara, . . . let's finish chapter three today; that's the one in which the mystery of the theft is solved. All right?

WOMAN: I can't. I don't want to. I can't bear this anymore.

MAN: So think of something else.

WOMAN: I just want to sit in silence.

MAN: Silence is our enemy. I've explained that hundreds of times. Besides, remember what you yourself said at the beginning.

WOMAN: I know what I said.

MAN: You said, "All these thoughts are driving me out of my mind. Out of my mind." Words—and I've said this a hundred times—are our salvation.

WOMAN: I don't want to talk. I don't want you to talk. Please, Artur.

MAN: All right. Let's be silent.

(Quiet. The MAN *whispers something. Two more shots are heard.)*

MAN: My God! What's that?

WOMAN: They're shooting people—nothing unusual.

MAN: They've both run out of the house. They're talking to each other, waving their hands. The farmer's run to the gate; he's pointing at the forest. He's shouting something.

Something's happened there. . . . Something's happened. My God, Klara, . . . the farmer's coming back. He's kicking a stone. He's angry. He's spitting. He's spitting. The woman's gone over to him; he's said something to her. She's crossed herself. That means somebody's been killed. You hear that? Somebody's been killed. They're nearby. *(He crosses over to the* WOMAN, *grabs her by the arm.)* Don't just lie there! Get hold of yourself!

WOMAN: You're hurting me.

MAN: I'm sorry. I didn't mean to. Maybe he'll come and tell us what happened. You know, when they found that bunker in the forest, he came and told us. Maybe he'll come tonight. Or maybe not for another couple of days. He's supposed to bring bread and milk the day after tomorrow.

WOMAN: You wanted to start the third chapter of the novel.

MAN: Don't be mean.

WOMAN: I'm just making a suggestion.

(A long silence.)

MAN: I know it bothers you that I have to keep talking. I didn't used to say much. I know. That's bound to be very irritating to someone who doesn't understand that it's the only way, that only words . . .

WOMAN: I do understand.

MAN: I'll take a look. . . . Nothing's happening. The yard's empty. There's a pile of manure in the right-hand corner. Not a hen in sight. Too bad. You know, I've gotten to like those hens. Maybe because I've gotten to know them a little better. I know their quirks; I know each one of them individually. For instance, the crested one was sad today. That's odd. Why would a hen be sad? I wouldn't mind being a hen. A hen, the farmer's dog, the farmer, anything but myself. . . . So, Sally Brown goes to see her uncle. Her fate will be determined that very day. Let's begin with a description of the morning. It promises to be a beautiful day. The sun rises over the forest, the dew beads up on the grass, it glistens, it glitters, it sparkles. . . . I'm sorry, it just slipped out. You have to admit that lately I've stopped trying to come up with synonyms. Right—the dew is glistening on the grass, it sparkles. . . . And the birds are beginning their merry morning song. First the oriole.

WOMAN: Why the oriole?

MAN: Just because.

WOMAN: There was an oriole who used to sing in our garden.

MAN: Klara, no memories. Remember our bargain.

WOMAN: You think that will help? I remember that oriole. It used to wake us up at six o'clock exactly. But I never saw it.

MAN: It promises to be a beautiful day, the sun rises over the forest, the dew is glistening on the grass, and the birds . . .

WOMAN: I'll tell you something. On the day of our wedding my mother came into the room and said, "It promises to be a beautiful day."

MAN: Please don't . . .

WOMAN: Her eyes were full of tears. I asked, "Why are you crying, Mama?" And she said, "That's how it is in this world; all mothers cry when their daughters get married." *(She cries.)*

MAN: You see. Why are you . . . ?

WOMAN: I dreamed about our daughter. I dream about her every night—

MAN: I wonder what that shot meant. Maybe they were just firing their guns. The farmer didn't look worried. But his wife crossed herself.

WOMAN: And it's always the same dream. She's running—

MAN: *(Putting his eye to the crack and speaking quickly.)* The yard is empty. Nothing has happened. Not a thing. There's a bird sitting on the fence.

(Sound of rain, wind, trees.)

MAN: Are you asleep, Klara?

WOMAN: No.

MAN: Do you hear? It's raining. It's raining, sprinkling, showering, pouring. It's drizzling. . . . I'm sorry, Klara. . . . Autumn's coming early this year.

(Sound of rain, wind, trees.)

MAN: I heard a knocking in the night.

WOMAN: Who was knocking? Who? Where?

MAN: A bird. It wasn't knocking so much as pecking. *Peck, peck.* It was walking on the roof right above our heads and going *peck, peck* with its beak. Rhythmically, carefully, sharply. As if it wanted to say, Open up, it's me. Or, I'm cold, let me in.

WOMAN: Are you sure it was a bird?

MAN: What else could it have been?

WOMAN: I don't know . . . I don't know . . .

MAN: I also heard a cry. Someone cried out. Far away. I don't know if it was a person or an animal. . . . And just before dawn a hay wagon rolled by on the road. Its wheels were rattling away merrily. When you think of hay wagons you always think of something happy, right? Maybe because you think of hay, and hay's the same color as the sun. They were probably heading out to the field to bring in the grain so it wouldn't get wet. Because right afterward it started pouring.

(Sound of rain.)

MAN: And since then it's been raining, drizzling, sprinkling, pouring, showering, driving. . . . What other words could you use, Klara?

(Long silence.)

MAN: I'm sorry. . . . And you were asleep. I could hear the rhythm of your breathing.

WOMAN: I dreamed about her again. I dream about her every night.

MAN: Sit down. . . . Sit down in front of the crack, take a look at the farmyard, take a deep breath. It smells—

WOMAN: And it's always the same. She's running along the road and cries out, Mama.

MAN: I'll talk to the farmer. Maybe he'll let us come down at night. Just for a minute. Although I have to admit he's right—that wouldn't be smart. Their children might see us, just by chance, or else hear something. No, I won't ask, we'll just have to . . . Klara, get up! You have to move around, just a little. It's very important. You'll wind up paying for all these months of immobility, and the price won't just be physical. We have to . . . just a little, Klara. A few deep breaths. Inhale, exhale.

WOMAN: *(She laughs mockingly.)* Inhale . . . exhale . . . Artur, you really are . . . *(She laughs louder and louder.)*

MAN: Quiet. Stop it, they'll hear you. Stop that! Someone will hear you, Klara!

WOMAN: Are you so afraid?

(Rain.)

WOMAN: Always the same dream. I don't dream of anyone else. Not my parents, not your brother Elek, not Aunt

Regina and her son. Nobody. How did it happen, Artur? If I hadn't let go of her hand . . . She saw a cat. "Mama, a little cat! On the wall, a little cat!" She said that, and then she was gone. Artur, do you remember how it happened? Because I don't . . . I don't remember anything.

MAN: Klara . . . Klara . . . my dear . . . how about a game of geography. We haven't played that in a long time. All right? Come on, please. You know the rules: three cities in one breath. Letter *B*. You start. Come on. Please.

WOMAN: *(Reluctantly.)* Barcelona.

MAN: Go on.

WOMAN: Barcelona. You have a cheerful nature, Artur.

MAN: Cheerful? You're being cruel. I don't deserve . . .

WOMAN: Exercise the body, exercise the mind, describe a morning, conjugate Latin verbs. Keep our life in order. What life? At first I really admired you, but later . . . I don't even know when . . . later you began to get on my nerves.

MAN: Barcelona, Bern, Buenos Aires . . .

WOMAN: You get on my nerves, you hear? You get on my nerves!

MAN: *(Whispering.)* Barcelona, Bern, Buenos Aires, Brussels, Baghdad, Burgos . . . Barcelona, Bern, Buenos Aires, Barcelona, Barcelona, Barcelona . . .

MAN: *(Looking through the crack.)* The sky is pale blue. The ground is covered with leaves. Autumn's coming early this year. The farmer's dog is walking around the yard. And one hen. The one who always keeps to herself. The solitary hen. The dog is chasing the hen. I can't see them. The door to the stable is propped open with a metal stick. It looks like they've gone out to the field. There are some wheelbarrows in front of the stable. The dog's chased away the hen and has sat down in front of the house. Want to take a look? . . . Three cars drove by last night. Probably trucks. We never used to hear any trucks. Maybe that means something. Maybe there's some movement on the front. Did you hear? Maybe they're planning some kind of operation in the forest against the partisans.

WOMAN: I heard them. You were talking to yourself all night.

MAN: I was trying to reconstruct *De bello Gallico* word for word. I used to be good at Latin. I've forgotten everything. Nothing but blanks. Then I tried to remember various proverbs. I managed to remember twenty-three proverbs.

WOMAN: She's running along and cries out, Mama!

MAN: I also finished a chapter of our novel, which begins with a description of the morning and Sally Brown's arrival at her uncle's. Would you like to hear it? *(Recites.)* It promises to be a beautiful day; the sun rises over the forest; the dew beads up on the grass.

WOMAN: No . . . no . . . please . . .

MAN: You touched my face? It's been so long . . . you never . . . oh, Klara . . .

WOMAN: Don't be angry. Give me your hand; hold me. I'm tired, I'm going to sleep.

WOMAN: I can't sleep. It's so hot in here.

MAN: You did sleep. I sat next to you, holding your hand. You slept a long time. The sun's already going down. It's getting dark. The air must be wonderful. A gentle sunset, a quiet sunset, a pale sunset . . . I'm sorry, dear.

WOMAN: It's all right, Artur. Go on and talk, I know it helps you, I know you have to . . .

MAN: A pale sunset. Can you remember any poem about a sunset?

WOMAN: A poem about a sunset? The sun was setting when they killed our parents.

MAN: *Darkness thickens on the grass*
An earthy wind blows cool
It seems the far horizon
Is coming close to you

WOMAN: These days you'd have to say "coming after you." The far horizon is coming after me. You know when I first read that poem? The Germans were marching into the city; we all went into the basement, except I didn't want to; I stayed upstairs. I was very afraid. So to calm myself I grabbed a book out of the library, just by chance. Suddenly I heard children running down the street. They cried out, "The Germans are coming! On motorcycles!" I went over to the window. The city was quiet, very calm and very beautiful. It was never like that. And then this terrible rumbling broke the silence. . . . I felt dizzy.

MAN: That same night I took you to the hospital.

WOMAN: That's right. And when you found out I had given birth to a daughter, you told the doctor, "We're so lucky it's not a boy." Just a minute ago, while I was sleeping, I dreamed about her again. No, this time it wasn't her. . . . It was me. This time it was me who was running and crying out something, and suddenly a big wall loomed up in front of me and blocked the road. I couldn't get across. I tried and tried, in vain. That's right, now I remember exactly, that's what I dreamed.

MAN: You're tired, Klara. Rest your head on my shoulder.

WOMAN: We're so lucky it's not a boy. . . .

MAN: Don't think about that, don't talk about it. You promised. . . . Oh, look, a flash of light. Another car on the road. Isn't that strange, so many cars in the last twenty-four hours? I'll ask the farmer. He's coming tomorrow. He's bringing bread and milk.

WOMAN: What was it he shouted, Artur?

MAN: Who?

WOMAN: You know, the one who killed her.

MAN: Don't talk. Let's just lie here quietly. Listen, the farmer's dog is barking.

WOMAN: What was it?

(The man doesn't answer.)

WOMAN: What was it?

MAN: *Die Eltern heraustreten.*

WOMAN: That's it. I couldn't remember what it was in German. *Die Eltern heraustreten.* He wanted the parents to step forward.

MAN: She was already dead, Klara.

WOMAN: I know. And we left her there by the wall, right where she spotted the cat. The cat got away. Frightened out of its mind, poor thing. We got away, too, didn't we?

MAN: That was later, Klara, much later.

WOMAN: I know that that was later. But we did get away. You and I.

MAN: He killed her.

WOMAN: And if he hadn't killed her, if she had gone on with us, with the rest of us? You and I wouldn't have been able to get away. She was small, she couldn't run fast. And she didn't understand. . . . Isn't it true that if she had gone with us, we wouldn't have been able to get away?

MAN: Klara, you know that they shot everybody in the ravine. Remember what the farmer said? Nobody else survived.

WOMAN: Answer me.

MAN: Calm down, my love, think about what . . .

WOMAN: Answer me.

MAN: No. We wouldn't have.

(Birdsong.)

MAN: Klara, listen! Do you hear? An oriole. Listen. The same throaty voice. It woke me up. Just like the old days. Klara! Klara! Klara? The farmer's coming today, he's bringing bread and milk. *(His voice betrays his growing despair.)* Klara? Klara, where are you? Klara . . .

(Birdsong suddenly grows quiet.)

MAN: It promises to be a beautiful day, the sun rises over the forest, the dew is glistening on the grass, sparkling, shimmering, glistening, glistening . . .

SABINA UNDER THE SACKS

Sabina was tall and thin, with a startled expression, as if she knew in advance that the world and its inhabitants had nothing good in store for her. Her eyes were an intense sky blue, the color of wild forget-me-nots—wild, not the paler garden variety—a blue you noticed right away. She inherited that color from her father. Her hair was thin, lanky, and limp. Once, when she tried on her Viennese sister's straw hat, everybody thought she looked like an English lady at the Ascot Derby. No one in the family had ever been to Ascot; they recognized the similarity thanks to photos in the magazine *Die Bühne*, to which they subscribed. Apparently the English ladies in the photographs were flat and thin like Sabina; they had light-colored eyes and wore gigantic hats. Sabina accepted this compliment with a startled expression. She lived with her parents in a small town in Galicia, where she spent her entire life, not counting the period of her marriage in Lvov, which ended in less than two years, when she unexpectedly returned home with a six-month-old baby and two large suitcases.

That marriage, it should be noted, had been arranged by a highly regarded local matchmaker; at the time Sabina was twenty years old. Her return was preceded by a letter from her husband, Paul, who worked as a clerk in a bank. Sabina's father read the letter and sat at the table a long time, lost in thought. Then he folded the paper into quarters and slipped it into his wallet. He was a dignified man with impeccable manners, slim and tall. Sabina had inherited not only the color of his eyes but his slim figure and height as well. He was also intelligent, pious, and respectful of tradition. Even so, he treated his children with a tolerance that was rare for those days; consequently they lived according to their own views and convictions. He wore a short, pointed beard.

"Who's the letter from?" asked his wife, a plump cushion of a woman, as kind as her husband but not nearly so intelligent.

"From Sabina's husband. She's coming back. The marriage is over."

Betty gasped. "Why? What happened?"

"Incompatibility."

"That's impossible! Sabina's such a quiet girl, so agreeable, so calm. . . ."

"It's not important. It doesn't matter. 'Incompatibility' is just a term to make the divorce proceedings easier. The marriage is over—and that's that. Please don't get upset, Betty. Remember your heart condition."

He rode to the station to meet his daughter, and on the way back he probed very gently. She didn't want to answer his questions. The buggy was clattering. The child, a little girl, was crying. She had the eyes of her mother and grandfather.

"He wasn't good to you?"

"Yes."

"Was it true what he wrote?"

"He beat me."

"I'm asking, was it true?"

Their eyes met. Sabina stared back at her father without answering. He didn't insist any further.

They rode on in silence until they reached the town. At that point Jakub W. stroked his daughter's hair, which had been limp and thin ever since she was a girl. Then he bent over the crying child and smiled as he said, *"Ein süsses Kind"*—"A sweet child"—in the language he used with Betty, an avid reader of Viennese romances.

Betty was waiting on the threshold; her cheeks were flushed. She burst into tears at the sight of her daughter with the baby. "My dear child, maybe it will work out somehow. Sometimes in a marriage there are—"

"No, Mama. I'm not going back to him. Ever."

Sabina's tone was curt. No one had ever heard her speak so forcefully.

During supper they talked about the child, who finally fell asleep, exhausted from crying. At one point Sabina's mother—her face still red—asked her daughter, "Why are you looking like that?"

"Like what?" asked Sabina.

Betty couldn't explain what she meant, but it was

obvious that she was talking about Sabina's new startled expression, which stayed with her for the rest of her life.

They went to bed early. Betty took a double dose of sleeping powder and lay on the mound of pillows until her heart stopped racing. She thought, Jakub will take care of everything; he'll figure things out somehow. And that soothing thought calmed her so that she was able to sleep.

Her husband got out of bed, opened the shutters, moved the armchair beside the window, and lit a cigarette. A moth flew into the room and fluttered under the shade of the night-light. Betty kept the window closed at night. She was afraid of nocturnal insects and the squeaking bats that circled low over the ground. He listened. Sabina's room was quiet.

She's a poor child, and I'm an old fool. Why did I have to go and marry her off to that pompous idiot? "Refused to fulfill her conjugal duties." Duties! Poor Sabina . . . and I wanted the best for her. She's so unlike her sisters, the only one—he didn't hesitate to think it—who didn't make anything of herself. But that he would beat her, no—that never would have occurred to me.

He sat for a long time, ruminating: he spent much of his life ruminating, which was why he hadn't accomplished more; he leased a small sawmill outside of town, near the forest. Every day he rode there in the buggy, sitting bolt upright, with his hands resting on the silver knob of his cane, smiling beneficently.

The day after his daughter returned, Jakub W., driving back from the mill, stopped at the house of a lawyer who was his friend. The two men talked for hours. The divorce proceedings went smoothly and hardly involved Sabina, who only had to sign a few papers in the lawyer's office. After the divorce Sabina showed no signs of relief, which is not to say that she didn't feel any. She never showed her feelings, not even with her child—no kisses or caresses in front of other people—unlike her father, who took every opportunity to demonstrate his affection for his granddaughter, albeit somewhat shyly and reservedly.

(How little we know about the real Sabina! We don't even know if there was a "real" Sabina. It's shameful, but true: she floats past the edges of our memory, here one minute, gone the next, never calling attention to herself or asking us to pay her any mind. Only her last moments, or more precisely the hours between dawn and dusk of her last day, have etched a permanent picture in my mind. And even these I did not witness myself; I only heard about them, just by chance. In that picture of her final hours, Sabina and her daughter, Dora, lie hidden under a pile of empty sacks in a corridor of the Judenrat. In a moment a drunken SS man will come bursting in. . . .)

A narrow stream flows sluggishly, monotonously, through the town. Sabina's life was like that stream.

She lived with her parents, helped out a little around the house—only a little, because Betty didn't want to dismiss the loyal woman who had been preparing her meals for years. She took care of her child, went to the library to borrow romances for her mother and, occasionally, books for herself. She wasn't very choosy; over time she devoured everything she laid her hands on—from Vicky Baum to Dostoyevsky. On market days she would buy butter wrapped in a cabbage leaf, without checking to see if it was fresh as all the other women did; she would toss fruits and vegetables into her basket. Her flat, angular figure stood out among the stately matrons religiously performing their ritual shopping. Her dress stood out as well; she always wore the elegant clothes she got from her sisters in Vienna, even to do the marketing, and she wore them the same way she bought things, carelessly, haphazardly, as if they were nothing special. They just hung on her like clothes on a hanger. The kinder people maintained that she had a certain nonchalant elegance—despite herself, of course. After all, what did Sabina care about elegance?

In the summer the Viennese sisters—already married, their studies completed, one had even received her doctorate—arrived from the grand world of theater and opera. The apartment was turned upside down, and the air was thick with the scent of new perfumes. You absolutely must find some kind of work, they told Sabina; they also told her she absolutely must read Karl Kraus and—of course—Thomas Mann, at least *The Magic Mountain*. Their father whispered, *"Lasst sie doch in Ruh"*—"Leave her in peace." Sabina looked worried.

Sabina enjoyed her sisters' visits. She wasn't envious of them—she didn't know what envy was. Still, when they left, she sighed with relief.

And when, just once, she went with her father to the city

of theater and opera, she came back disappointed. She discovered that her sisters lived as modestly as newlyweds, that they worked from morning to night, that they stood in line at the box office for two hours to get an opera ticket, and then stood for three more on the highest balcony. On Sundays they strapped on their backpacks and went on an outing. They also went to meetings. One sister was a Socialist, the other a Zionist; one thought in red, the other in blue and white. Occasionally, they argued with each other furiously. Sabina's own sympathies were more blue-white.

Little Dora went to school. When she came back, she asked, "Where is my father? Why am I the only one in the class who doesn't have a father?" (The bank clerk had disappeared without a trace.) Until one day she found a solution: "I told the girls that Grandfather Jakub is my father."

Dora was big, ungainly, ugly. Later she surprised everyone with her milky-pink, dreamy complexion. That was already during the period when the transports to Belzec were leaving one after the other, and there was great fear and great hunger. During meals—either bread or barley meal or millet—Dora would raise her eyes, and when she did, her milky-pink face was blissful.

She was ten years old when her grandfather Jakub took sick. He lay in his bed, his face covered with a black salve: they told her he had Saint Anthony's fire. She was perplexed and asked whether there really was such a thing as black fire. The black face on the white pillowcase scared her.

With his pointed goatee, Grandfather Jakub looked like the devil. When he asked her to come closer, she ran away. The black fire killed her grandfather.

After her husband's death Betty refused to leave the apartment and read fewer and fewer romances. She would sit on the balcony in her armchair, wearing a black dress with a lace ruffle around her neck, majestic and kind as she looked down from the third story onto the courtyard gardens and the white goats nibbling at the scruffy lawn.

Without looking or asking for it, Sabina found work—it landed in her lap. Her new job was voluntary and consisted of collecting the monthly dues from the members of Wizo, the Zionist women's organization to which she herself belonged. Each month she went from house to house, writing out receipts, and twice a year—at Hanukkah and Purim—she helped organize appropriate entertainment for the evening festivities.

More often she sat at the entrance to some room specially rented for the purpose and sold tickets. This humble activity was important to her—it was her entire social life. When asked about her "work," Sabina would liven up; otherwise, she didn't have much to say. And, as always, she retained her startled expression.

Once during the annual Purim ball a stranger walked up to Sabina while she was selling tickets and asked her to dance.

"I don't dance," she replied, truthfully. Her voice shook.

"In that case would you join me for coffee?"

The local orchestra was playing a waltz by Strauss, and Sabina had the strange impression that the entire unreal scene had been lifted straight out of one of her mother's romances.

"I can't right now"—her voice quavered lightly—"because the guests are still coming in, but in half an hour I'd be happy to have a cup of coffee."

"So I'll come kidnap you in half an hour," the man replied, then disappeared. After he left, Sabina was in turmoil: she sat motionless, staring into space, with an expression more startled than usual, as if she knew in advance that the world and its inhabitants had nothing good in store for her. Her reverie ended abruptly when she spotted her neighbor, Sara the manicurist, hurrying down the hall. Sara's face was pale, and she was clutching her unbuttoned coat. Without stopping she called out, "Quick, Sabina. Hurry."

Sabina raised her hand to her mouth and stifled a cry.

At home she found Dora cowering on the edge of the couch, mute with terror. In the bedroom, high up on the mound of pillows, lay her mother—dead.

The Viennese sisters did not attend their mother's funeral. At the time they were cleaning sidewalks and toilets in the city of theater and opera under the supervision of the Gestapo. They wrote letters saying: "Escape. Move to Palestine. We'll meet there." They managed to leave Europe just before the war. Dora had been learning Hebrew for a long time, which—considering the fervor with which Sabina worked at Wizo, as well as her own Zionist sympathies—suggests that Sabina had some plans of her own. When the war broke out, the Russians occupied the town, and Sabina survived nearly two years of Russian occupation without a scratch—and without a job: she lived modestly off the inheritance from her parents.

When the Germans marched in, she fell into a panic and was paralyzed with fear.

They survived the first *Aktion*, and the second by hiding—but not the third.

Many years—decades—after the war, it was discovered, just by chance . . .

("Just by chance". . ."not until decades later"—these phrases keep coming back, so many footnotes to specific fates.)

It was known that they were taken away early in the morning, just after the SS had begun the *Aktion* in the town surrounded by Einsatzkommando troops. They were taken and locked up with others in the public bathhouse. It was known that the trucks drove up at dusk, and that the train headed for Belzec later that night: its whistle blew as it pulled out of the station. That much was known.

But the picture of Sabina and Dora inside a corridor of the Judenrat, underneath a pile of empty sacks that once held flour used to bake a coarse bread—that was not known for decades.

Not until decades after the war, when the memory of

that time was reignited (contrary to its usual habit), did a tourist from Australia, encountered just by chance, unveil that particular picture.

He was the only one who could have unveiled it, because he, too, was lying under a pile of sacks in the exact same corridor, just as they were, only in a different corner, to the right of the entrance, out of the SS man's line of sight. And they were lying on the left. How overwhelming Sabina's despair must have been, like a blaze of mad, blind energy. How difficult it must have been for her to force her way to the hole knocked out of the bathhouse wall just above the ground—a small hole, few people could have fit through it—dragging Dora behind her and gripping her hand tightly, since it was Dora she wanted to save, *Dora*, and not herself. That's certain.

The Australian, once their fellow townsman, now heavy and gray but at that time young and nimble, crawled through the hole in the wall right behind them and ran after them until all three reached the Judenrat, which was nearby. The corridor was empty save for two huge piles of sacks.

There they lay in their corners, invisible under the sacks. They heard someone running past them, someone shouting, someone calling someone else. . . .

A drunken SS man (we know he was drunk because of his ranting and raving) burst in and in his drunken rage kicked the pile of sacks. Whoever he hit—mother? daughter?—failed to stifle a groan. He kicked apart the pile of bags, dragging mother and daughter into the light of day or, to be more precise, of evening, since the day was already ending, and chased them back to where they had escaped from that morning. You could already hear the whirring of the motors on the trucks.

I rarely thought about Sabina. But lately I think of her more and more.

NOCTURNAL VARIATIONS ON A THEME

He was freed from the camp and passed through the gate with the sign ARBEIT MACHT FREI. He was overcome by a wave of happiness unlike any he had ever known.

Beyond the gate the asphalt road stretched out, flat and empty, as far as the horizon. He started walking down the empty asphalt road with a light, almost winged step. A pale sun shone in the pale sky.

Suddenly, from far away, he spotted a figure running toward him. At first he couldn't make out who it was. Only when the distance between them had diminished did he recognize the girl he loved. She was running to meet him. Her hair was streaming in the wind.

It wasn't long until she—radiant, smiling—fell into his arms. "Do you have a cigarette?" she asked, breathless from running. He froze. He remembered that he had left his cigarettes on his cot back in the camp, and he realized that in order to fulfill the wish of the girl he loved, he had to go back. And so he did.

He was freed from the camp and passed through the gate with the sign ARBEIT MACHT FREI. He was overcome by a wave of happiness unlike any he had ever known.

Beyond the gate was a new-growth forest. He started walking down the path with a light, almost winged step past the trees, bushes, and ferns, while the moon lit his way with its white glow.

Suddenly he looked up and noticed that the sky above him was moonless and black, and he understood: the light which had lit his way was the searchlight from the watch-tower, which had followed him and had now caught him in its beam. He realized that he had to go back to the camp. And so he did.

He was freed from the camp and passed through the gate with the sign ARBEIT MACHT FREI. He was overcome by a wave of happiness unlike any he had ever known.

Beyond the gate the asphalt road stretched out, flat and empty, as far as the horizon. He started walking down the empty asphalt road with a light, almost winged step. A pale sun shone in the pale sky. He kept walking and lost all track of time. Suddenly he saw a turnstile blocking the road. A white sign with an arrow indicated a detour. He obediently followed the arrow and kept on going with a light step along an asphalt road that looked remarkably like the one he had just left. He kept walking and lost all track of time, until another turnstile blocked his way. Here, too, the arrow was pointing to the right. He stopped and looked around: nothing, emptiness, pale sun in pale sky. He started off in the direction indicated by the arrow. He kept walking and lost all track of time until he saw ahead of him the gate with the sign ARBEIT MACHT FREI. In front of the gate stood an SS man, who crooked his finger and beckoned him over.

THE HAND

Why choose this to write about? After all, I've been subjected to every conceivable form of maltreatment and abuse. Maybe because this was the last blow, and therefore the most painful—I don't know. At the time, I was lying on the hard, frozen ground, looking up at the bare trees and whispering to myself, You idiot, you stupid old fool. But that didn't stop my heart from aching: it's aching still today, even though I lived through two years of hell, and I understand that within each of us there is a limit to what we know about ourselves.

Back then, in the beginning, I was still very disciplined and strong enough to haul sacks of cement. I kept myself scrupulously clean—as if the threat of death weren't constantly lurking at my side—and managed to avoid the ubiquitous diarrhea, eczema, and even typhus. During roll call, when we all stood naked in the biting frost, I imagined being caught by a sudden nightfall in the mountains, two thousand meters above sea level, and my skinny body managed to survive. I was managing, all right, back then, at least in the beginning, despite the hard labor and the fact that the two years in the concentration camp had taken their toll.

The SS man swung his rifle butt. The sack fell from the boy's back, and we had to carry him away. His mouth was bleeding. He was so young he could have been my son; as we carried him, he looked like a big child in pain.

I visited Jaro in the infirmary and brought him bread; it probably would have stopped there if I hadn't discovered that we shared a common passion.

I remember how he spoke to me, with the stubbornness of a child determined to keep his promise: "I'm going to get the hell out of here—and then you'll see. I'm going to make it up the southern slope of Mount Zamarla!"

I felt as if a wind had suddenly blown in from the Tatra Mountains and was shaking me from head to toe. I felt twenty years younger, just like that. I must have stared at him a little strangely, because he started to explain himself.

Later on, Jaro moved to my bunk. I showed him how to carry sacks, how to breathe so as to put the least strain on his heart; I acquainted him with the complicated social hierarchy of the camp, taught him self-defense tactics, and warned him not to eat potato peels and to inspect himself for lice. He was very young and very new.

In our barracks in the evening the others would sometimes laugh at us and say, "There go those two crazy trekkers again."

And trek we did, systematically, according to plan, beginning from the Bielski Tatras all along the entire ridge up to Krywan. We rationed the peaks and took them in small increments, trying out every variant of the ascents we knew about from our own experience or from guidebooks. It was amazing how much he knew for someone only eighteen years old. And he talked about the mountains like a teenager in love, with a light in his eye and a catch in his voice. My own passion, which age and suffering had turned to ashes, was rekindled by those evenings and burned hotter and brighter than before, fueled by a longing impossible to fulfill. On more than one night I dreamed of the slopes, of hiking through cool, dark valleys with roaring streams. We covered scraps of paper with thick zigzags that came together at the summit. I gazed at the jumble of lines so long I could feel the granite in my fingers, and even my legs, feeble and thin as sticks, stiffened from the effort. I don't know about him, only half my age, but for me those moments were nourishing, healing—they were salvation. For the soul, of course; my body had deteriorated so that I scarcely looked human.

Over time our silences became more and more frequent; our pauses, our moments of reflection, became longer. In the end the only words left were the absolutely necessary everyday phrases and camp jargon.

We never finished our trek.

But he still shared my bunk, where now and then a nightmare made him grope for my hand. In my thoughts I called him son.

That winter they evacuated us to M. The icy mountain wind was blowing down the road above the quarry; on the far horizon a blue-black wavy line was visible. I don't remember whether I realized those waves were the Alps.

Now Jaro was no longer saying he was going to get the hell out. Now he said that a human being was just a fly, and any old shoe could come along and crush it.

We realized then that it was a matter of days. At night the sky was filled with light, and the earth shook. It was a matter of days, and it would be awful to stand on the threshold like that and not make it through.

They chased us out during the night, amid confusion, shots, and the groans of the dying. They hurried us, a handful of half-dead Muselmänner off the roads and through the forest; no one doubted this would be our last journey. Our bodies grew prematurely stiff, and our skin turned purple beneath our striped rags.

Jaro stayed with me. "Hold me," he whispered. His hand and the cold are all I remember of that night.

Before sunrise we came to a spot in the woods that had recently been cleared. Apart from the one SS guard booth, there was only a small windowless shed with one entrance, encircled by barbed wire. The earth inside the shed had been packed down by human feet—we were not the first ones there.

We walked in single file through the narrow door, collapsing onto one another, utterly fatigued and barely conscious. Standing, we all might have managed to fit, but who was in any condition to stand even for a second?

I felt the end was near. The night march, my heart . . . it was a miracle I hadn't been left by the road like so many others.

Squashed by my fellow prisoners, I sat with my legs bunched up; my back rested against Jaro's bony knee: he was sitting propped against the wall.

Two days passed. Not a drop of water, not a slice of bread. Just the SS guards with their rifles, the safeties released. Why didn't they finish us off? To save bullets? Was it that they knew we'd die anyway, in two or three days? In the night the sky was on fire; shots echoed throughout the woods; freedom was right there—and we were powerless, a useless heap of dry twigs.

On the evening of the second day, Jaro moved. I felt some space open up behind me and went tumbling backward—I was lying down! Oh, the happiness of that moment of relief! Jaro crawled toward the door, while the others cursed him, since he was crawling over them, over the tangle of human bodies, not yet dead but only half alive. They didn't let me lie there for more than few seconds—they ordered me to move and sit up. Every centimeter was a matter of life and death. It took a great deal of effort for me to make my way over to the wall. Then I was drained. I grew faint and began breathing heavily. I don't know how long it was before I heard Jaro's voice saying, "Move! That's my place!"

He was right. It was his place, a better place because it was next to the wall. He was also right to demand it back, even though he was just eighteen years old: we were all equal in the face of death. I whispered, "Give me a second to gather my strength."

He must not have heard me, because he shouted at me one more time—and then he started pounding away at me.

"Jaro," I whispered. "Just a minute, I'm moving. . . ." But he went on hitting me, and finally he threw himself on top of me.

"You animal," he shouted. "Get out of here. That place is mine!"

He kept beating me for a long time before he squeezed beneath me. Now I was lying on top of him, and the others were shouting that they were suffocating, because suddenly there was even less space all around us, and no one could breathe. But who cared about them?

I saw Jaro's eyes, alive inside a dead face, and I saw the hatred in those eyes.

He shoved me off: I was amazed by his strength and asked myself where it came from. Now I was lying on top of somebody else. There wasn't a single centimeter of empty space all around me, though just a minute earlier there had been room for my body, too. I crawled toward the exit, trampling the others—I, who hadn't had the strength to move a muscle. As if Jaro's kicks and blows, as if Jaro's hand upon me, had unleashed what little will to live I still had left.

I leaned on the door and stood up. The sky was full of stars, the ground covered with frost. The trees were slender and bare. I stood there for a while until my lungs got used to the sharpness of the air, then I took a few steps forward and lay down on the ground.

A few months later, on my way back home after a long stay in the hospital, I stopped in P. My train wasn't leaving until evening, so I walked around town, still very weak and full of anxiety about the fate of my loved ones.

A man was walking a few meters ahead of me; the hair was just beginning to grow back on his head. I passed him without recognizing him. But he shouted my name and grabbed me in an embrace.

He was wearing a checked sports shirt; I could tell he'd already regained weight. He didn't let go of me for a long time. He laughed, and I saw the gap in his smile where the guard in the quarry had knocked out his two front teeth.

"Brother," he cried out. "We made it! Remember what I told you back then? Let's go mountain climbing. What do you say?"

He grasped my shoulder—an ordinary gesture of friendship. I suddenly lost my breath; my vision clouded over. I pried his hand off my shoulder. I could feel his bewildered gaze on my back as I walked away.

AN ADDRESS

The telegram came at eight in the morning. He was still in bed; he didn't feel like getting up. He couldn't stand Sundays anymore; they were empty days, difficult to fill. So he stayed in bed as long as he could, waiting for the morning commotion to die down in the apartment and the scrambling for the bathroom and kitchen to cease. That usually took quite some time, since the apartment housed three families, one in each of three large rooms. He himself occupied only a tiny cubicle, probably a former maid's room; its only advantage was that it belonged exclusively to him. It didn't even have enough space for a second bed. One night, when some of the landlord's relatives from eastern Poland came to visit, he was obliged to share it with a ten-year-old boy. The boy slept on the floor.

That was probably the best night he had spent in that house; otherwise he slept fitfully, plagued by nightmares; he often woke in the middle of the night and lay awake until dawn. That night, as the "little" boy—he thought of him as a little boy, though in reality he was already quite large—

was lying on a mattress spread out next to his bed, he had the sensation that Julian had come back and fallen asleep, worn-out, still a little unfamiliar, a little more grown up, a little more of a man. He listened to the boy's breathing, looked at his dark head buried in the pillow. How easy it was to slide right into that trap so cunningly laid by his imagination!

He gave in to the emotion and, for the first time since he came back, felt a warmth welling up inside him. Embers long extinguished and covered with ashes once again caught fire. He began to thaw. That night he slept peacefully, more so than the boy, who tossed and groaned in his sleep. The morning was difficult. He avoided looking the boy in the eye when the boy grew talkative and curious and tried to engage him in conversation. He excused himself by saying he was in a hurry, and because, as always, there was a line for the bathroom, he left the house unwashed and unshaven, even more morose and withdrawn than usual. The fresh air calmed him down. He reproached himself severely for his momentary lapse into sentimentality, for departing from his cool and rational habit of mind. That evening he found his room had been tidied up; the landlady thanked him for his kindness and informed him that her relatives had left for Lower Silesia. He was relieved the boy had gone, but that night he slept very badly. Uncharacteristically, he took a strong dose of sleeping pills.

It would be madness to delude himself into believing that Maria and the boy were still alive. Seven months of tireless searching—letters, advertisements, trips to question acquaintances, and visits with strangers—and not a trace. Everything broke off on the tenth of May 1943. From numerous accounts and conversations, he was able to reconstruct practically every one of his wife and son's moves during the occupation—up to that day. Not a single link was missing: first Warsaw, the apartment on Hoza and the surname Wislowska. Then a move to Krakow under the name Kowalska; finally a return to Warsaw (he couldn't understand why they went back), the room at the engineer Z.'s, and a job at the post office.

On the tenth of May, Maria and the child left the house at eight in the morning. Nobody ever saw them again; nobody ever asked about them. After that there was only darkness and silence.

"I don't want to be cruel," said Z., the engineer, "but I think the only explanation is that they ran into some thug who denounced them."

"But it could have been a roundup! They could have been sent to a work camp!" he replied to all those who either shrugged their shoulders or else dismissed his crazy search for the dead as the pitiful act of a desperate man.

One month before the telegram he stopped looking. His suitcase was stuffed with replies, forms, and letters, all of which said no. There were official seals from the Red Cross, the White Cross, the Jewish Committees, the Office of Repatriation, Joint, HIAS, the cities of Warsaw, Geneva, London, Paris. One month before the telegram he locked his suitcase with a key and accepted the death sentence. He stopped asking, stopped chasing people, stopped collecting wartime biographies. He took a job in an office, where he soon earned a reputation as a conscientious—if unapproachable—colleague. He began writing "widower" whenever he filled out forms.

And then it came. His immediate impulse was to reach for a cigarette, but his hands shook so violently he couldn't light the match. So he collapsed back onto his pillow, weak and shaking, like someone barely recovered from a long illness.

"I knew it," he whispered. "I knew it."

The news came from the Warsaw branch of the Red Cross, which had more than once told him something entirely different from what that day's telegram said. Obviously Maria's address had taken this long to reach it. Letters from abroad take a long time; many disappear en route. So there wasn't any reason to be surprised. He kept holding the little white card close to his eyes, kept reading the crooked lines of type: "Maria Kranz with son camp UNRRA 94 Ettlingen Germany American Zone."

"Just as I thought. First a roundup, then a work camp or some other kind of forced labor. I knew they were alive."

He imagined the huge vaulted station in an unknown city, imagined himself stepping off the train, walking toward the two of them. Maria in the light dress he liked so much, her hands shading her eyes, and little Julian . . .

Julian had the same face and the same dark hair as the boy who had spent the night with him.

A salty drop slipped into his mouth. I'm crying, he thought with joy.

An hour later, as he was saying good-bye to his landlady,

he asked her to call his office and explain his sudden departure. "Couldn't you put it off until tomorrow?" she asked, surprised not so much by the news itself, which was common enough in those days, as by how fast things seemed to be going. "Prepare for your trip, buy provisions for the road; after all; it's a long way. Wouldn't it be better if you applied for an exit visa? If you try to cross without papers, you're likely to wind up in prison! Why don't you write your wife and ask her to come here? In a month the dining room will be free; the doctor and his family are moving in with his parents."

He listened politely, patiently, already equipped for his journey—a warm sweater, a knapsack, a windbreaker. Then he repeated, "The only thing I'd like you to do is call the office."

He acted efficiently, logically, decisively. He left the city on the first train headed southwest. After studying the map, he decided the best place to cross the border would be near one of the spa towns, where the heavily wooded plateau would provide the most security. Besides, it was silly to worry about danger at the very moment he had finally found his wife and son.

When he got off the train he hardly noticed the picturesque little town, its narrow streets and covered walkways. While he was waiting for the bus, he sat down in a smoky pub; through the dirty windowpanes he could see people milling near the kiosks in front of the railroad station.

He had calculated it to the moment. He would reach K.

at sunset, so he would have plenty of time to cross the border.

He bought cigarettes, rolls, and apples and tossed them into his knapsack.

Riding on the bus, he had the impression that the whole day was a dream from which he could not awake. Suddenly frightened, he must have moaned out loud, since his neighbor turned to look at him and asked in a thick Lvov accent: "Are you all right?"

When they reached the end of the line, he kept walking down the road; according to his map he had to go for two more kilometers before veering off into the forest.

In the evening he made good progress. The clean mountain air made it easier to breathe; his leg muscles felt supple and fit. Now he would be able to talk with Maria for as long as he wanted, all through the night and the whole next day. Now at last it would be possible. He never could talk to a Maria who had been murdered, a dead Maria.

The forest floor was fragrant and moist. He pushed on slowly, at the even pace of an experienced hiker; he didn't stop until he reached the summit. Full of quiet happiness, he gazed up at the sky and at the stars. He called out loudly, "Maria!"—and the echo answered.

He made it. After two days his eyes were burning, his legs swollen. He traveled by train, he traveled on foot—without seeing anything around him. He passed by famous cities with utter indifference. He completely ignored the sounds of a foreign language. He paid absolutely no attention to the fact that the country in which he found himself was enemy territory.

After two days, the land again began to rise in gentle green domes. There, at the foot of those hills, was Maria.

In the pub they were able to point him in the right direction. The UNRRA camp was located in the former SS barracks, some distance out of town, in the woods.

"Eine wunderbare Gegend"—a German woman sitting behind the counter praised the area. Her hair was freshly curled. The beer hall was chilly and neat; the wooden stools and benches gleamed, polished by the bottoms of the beer drinkers.

The German woman had blood-red fingernails; the radio was playing a Bach violin concerto. He left quickly, as if they were after him.

He passed the bridge and the last houses at the edge of the city. The day was ending; the cars racing past at full speed had already switched on their headlights.

Around the bend, against the backdrop of the forest, were several light-colored multistoried buildings.

He wanted to walk faster, but his heart wouldn't let him. He was panting as if he'd been running for miles. His legs felt weak; he knew it wasn't fatigue. He wiped his forehead; moist, dirty stains appeared on his handkerchief. Without stopping, he lit a cigarette.

He was afraid.

"Where do you think you're going?" a guard wearing an American uniform asked him in Polish. "The office is closed now."

Incoherently, he attempted to explain what he wanted

and that he couldn't wait until morning. Please, right now, right this minute . . .

He sat down on the steps and waited. Before him there was a large plaza surrounded by barracks now used as living quarters. The grass was dotted with women and children. Small groups of people strolled along the paths. Someone was playing an accordion. In the middle of the plaza stood a tall, thick flagpole flying the red-and-white Polish flag.

"Are you the one looking for Maria Kranz?" He heard a male voice above him. He nodded. His throat was dry, constricted. "Pani Maria is our nurse. She lives in the fourth building. Room number fifteen."

He thanked the man, flung his knapsack over his shoulder, and walked off without saying a word, even though the man was clearly waiting for some sort of explanation.

He sensed he was causing a stir; people were stopping to stare at him. He suddenly remembered he had neither shaved nor washed properly for three days. The dirt and grime had turned his windbreaker completely gray; his shoes were coated by a layer of dust.

In front of the entrance to the fourth building he stopped and took a deep breath. His heart hurt as he exhaled.

He climbed up to the second story, checked the number of the room next to the stairwell: ten. That meant her door was the fifth one down.

He couldn't bring himself to knock right away. He stood and listened. The room was quiet. A thin bar of light shone through the crack of the door. He wanted to call out her name, but his lips felt numb. He heard a door slam shut on the floor below, a female voice scolding, then the cry of a small child.

He gently turned the handle. The door opened softly, without resistance. Inside the room a lamp was burning, next to the bed. On the bed, wrapped in a gray blanket, lay a woman. A woman he'd never seen before.

He stood in the doorway and exhaled loudly. The woman raised her head. He saw her light hair, her very light hair, piled up in tiny curls. She was not young. He clutched at the last bit of hope, although he now knew it was in vain.

"I'm looking for Pani Kranz. Maria Kranz, and her son." Instinctively, he added, "I'm her husband."

The woman's eyes widened. She jumped up, then quickly regained control and said calmly, "There's been some mistake. My husband was killed. You must be looking for a different Maria Kranz."

He took two steps forward and, without taking off his knapsack, collapsed into a chair.

"What do you mean, a different Maria Kranz? What do you mean, a mistake? She's dead and you call it a mistake!"

She came closer. He saw the age, the weariness in her face.

"She was so young, so beautiful," he said. Then he added quickly, "I'm sorry. Please forgive me, I've gone for three days without—"

"There's nothing to forgive," she interrupted, shrugging

her shoulders. They stood there a moment in silence. Then she added, “Where did you get my address?”

He took the telegram from his pocket and handed it to her without a word. She read it and placed it on the table. He left it lying there.

“The Red Cross. Of course. I wrote them about a month ago—one last time, I thought. You see, I’m still hoping, too, that somebody from my family might. . . . Except I would have checked first, instead of packing my bags and taking off, just like that, just like a moth toward a flame. . . .”

What was there to check? he thought. The same exact name. With son. But he could only repeat, “Please forgive me. I’ll be on my way.”

He returned to the little town. His steps were heavy, labored. Everything hurts, he thought. One dull ache.

It was already dark. The streets were dead, deserted. Only the pub on the square where he had asked for directions was lit up. He was afraid he might not have the strength to walk there. He stopped and leaned against the stone wall around the fountain. One dull ache, he thought again, one great dull ache . . .

A young woman wearing a light dress came running out of the square, stepping lightly. She ran right by him, so close, so close—and disappeared into the dark. His heart pounded. He gripped his chest to calm it. He stood there clutching his heart and waited. She’ll come back. She’ll call my name. Like she did once.

The pub was empty. The waitress with the blood-red fingernails was reading a book. The radio was silent. He took off his knapsack, sank onto the bench, covered his face with his hands, and sat there motionless. Without waiting for his order, the German woman placed a full mug in front of him. He drank it down in one gulp.

"Sie fahren weg?"—"You're leaving?"—she asked as he paid for the beer. "That's a pity, it's no nice here . . . *eine wunderschöne Gegend.* . . . The tourists will soon return; our vineyards are famous throughout the country. . . . *Wein, Weib, und Gesang* . . ."—"wine, women, and song." He looked up, and his eyes frightened her; she stepped back.

The night was cool. He reached the station just as the green signal arm was going up. He climbed aboard the train, without knowing its destination, and took a seat beside the window, beyond which lay the thick, impenetrable darkness.

HENRYK'S SISTER

One hour ago I arrived in this large, prosperous, utterly foreign city. Four hours ago I hung up the receiver in a small inn, high in the mountains, a third-rate resort with a third-rate glacier usually shrouded by the fog that gathers all too readily above this village in its deep, narrow valley. Two weeks ago I was carefully avoiding the black phone perched on the table near the bottles of apple brandy, but today, one day before I am to return home (a journey across many borders), I gave in. My fingers trembled, trapped in the holes of the telephone dial; my voice shook when I said my last name, which is also hers.

Why didn't I say: You should come here to S., it takes three hours by train, there's only one inn here, the place is empty, the owner's name is Michel, if you look out the dining room windows you can see a third-rate glacier shrouded by fog or clouds, a dreary village in a prosperous country; people rarely come here, the buses only stop here for a moment, the tourists glance at the glacier hidden in the fog, down a glass of apple brandy, and drive on to some more colorful, cheerful place—after all there are plenty to choose from. I too came here by bus; it was raining, no sign of the glacier, but I stayed. Michel took care of me; I was his only guest. I slept poorly, your presence in the city only three hours away by train robbed me of my sleep. I suspect that that's the only reason I chose this country: no, not because of you, because of Henryk.

I should have said: Please come, we'll sit on the window seat by the big, rough country table; of course, of course, it brings back memories—we spent our last days together in the country.

"No, it's better at a café, in town—"

Michel looked at me anxiously. Was I shouting?

"—and best if it's someplace small, out of the way."

"What does 'out of the way' mean?" she asked.

"Someplace quiet, with not too many people."

"Fine, how about the Café Bel on the lake? It's deserted at that hour. But how will we recognize each other?"

The laugh caught in my throat, but I didn't say: You were twins, after all.

"I'll be holding a bouquet of violets," I said, and added quickly, "See you at eight, then." I put down the receiver, but I stayed close to the phone, wondering whether I should call her back and cancel.

"Ça va, madame?" Michel asked. He didn't understand the language in which we had spoken, but he understood that something was wrong.

I sat down near the window. A group of children was returning from a school outing; they kept their hoods up as they made their way through the drizzle back to the station. I asked for a glass of hot milk. *Ça va mieux?* In this part of the country they speak French. I should have met Henryk's sister here; language is bound to play a certain role in our meeting. *Sie wünschen bitte?* the waiter at the café will ask: What will you have? *Hände hoch, du Sauhund, du Dreck*—Hands up, you swine, you dog, you piece of filth—*Hände hoch, zweimal Kaffee bitte,* Two coffees, please, the aroma of espresso, the glare of neon lights, picking at a piece of cake with a delicate dessert fork . . . laughter.

The city is shining. I'm walking down the straight, wide main street along with the evening crowd. It's drizzling here, too. Like parachutes, the umbrellas bob above the city on their skinny handles, massing together in one great multicolored nylon sky; above this sky rise the treetops and, higher still, a second sky, the real sky, gray and cloudy.

The street runs down to the lake: I know, I saw it on the map. I ought to go down one of the side streets, into the old part of town where the colored lights along the riverfront paint the faces of the grand old houses.

Why did I call? We have a right to know the details; that's the least you can do for us, now, when . . . I tore up all the letters, but in vain: I remembered every word. So it was in vain, then, when I ran—in vain, because I'm still here. I'm alive.

I've already passed three florists—so colorful, so fragrant, their floral displays like altars. I closed my eyes as I passed the first and walked slower so that it would take longer to reach the next. The rain has let up; the nylon sky has metamorphosed into sharp colored spears hooked around wrists.

I stop at the fourth flower shop and stand on the threshold and ask.

Unfortunately, *gnädige Frau*, we don't have any violets; the season for violets has been over for a long time. The saleslady in a tight black dress offers me a polite smile and a bunch of roses. Must they be violets?

No, I say to myself as I walk on. The season's been over for a long time. They used to grow beneath our bedroom window, beneath the window. . . . In the first drugstore I come to I buy a little something for my nerves and gulp it down. If only it could be over and done with. How on earth will I tell her? Will I tell her anything at all?

We had moved to the country. Henryk was working in the forest. He was sunburned; no one ever asked him who he was until one Sunday, two months after we arrived, one Sunday, early in the morning, we were still asleep . . .

A green light. I walk onto the street, cross to the other side, but that doesn't change anything. Wherever I go the same thing awaits me, on this side or that, nothing changes, illusions of an escape that can never happen. It's getting dark, almost eight. I can't stop time, but I can make my feet go where I want. So why am I walking straight ahead? Why am I steering through the evening crowd toward the lake? There's more air. The street is growing wider. I can taste the nearness of the water.

. . . when suddenly we heard a pounding on the door, shaking the little house so that the seascape with its seagull and its sand dunes came crashing off the wall. The glass shattered. There was a brief silence, and again the pounding shook the rickety house. Henryk leaped up . . .

Bitte zwei—two bouquets of violets; I'll throw them in the lake. They look withered. The season's been over for a long time. They're so small, so plain.

. . . Henryk leaped up out of bed. I wondered what he was doing. He flung open the shutters, daylight flooded the room, the seascape glass shattered on the floor, he jumped out the window. . . .

And now, at last, the beautiful lake. The water's a deep, dark blue, my favorite color. Waves lap against the shore, rocking the boats. I already see the neon sign BEL; it's right there, much too close; I only have a few minutes left; the uneven click of my heels against the sidewalk, one strong, one weak. I'm limping as I run.

Out of breath, I stand beside a green fence enclosing ten little tables. Nobody's sitting at them. It's too cold to drink coffee outside. But inside, behind the huge pane of glass, in the muted light, in the plush old-fashioned interior . . .

A painful journey across women's faces, smooth and matte beneath the piled-up pyramids of hair, over thick lips, thin lips, around round or almond-shaped eyes, sunken or protruding, a painful journey in search of my quarry: the face of Henryk's sister. My glance skitters among the little tables, along the walls, undistracted by the clatter of teaspoons, the warm, safe aroma of coffee.

I didn't know it would hurt so literally: a pain in the heart, a sudden shortness of breath. Henryk's sister sits at the back of the room, underneath the window. But it's not her sitting there. It's Henryk, who has put on women's clothes for a joke, a two-piece tweed suit for the fun of it, and he's painted the nails of his beautiful long hands carmine. That's his high, prominent forehead, the sculpted, carved nose so typical of Jews and the people down south who live in the mountains. It's Henryk reincarnated as his beautiful sister.

My laugh sounds like a sneer and is a response to her own full, joyous laughter, which I cannot hear through the windowpane but which I can see. She's not alone. She's with a man, the opposite of Henryk, a well-fed, good-natured man who immediately places his plump hand on her thin one, perhaps to stop her from laughing.

We laugh—they behind the glass, and I in front of the green fence. I laugh, although I really should be serious and solemn, and even thank fate for letting me see Henryk's face one more time. That's a lot: for years I haven't been able to recall his face, no matter how hard I tried; I don't have any photographs, and the last picture in my mind erased everything else. Whenever I try to summon his face all that comes to mind is that last moment in the garden, right after he jumped out the window. The house was surrounded. *Hände hoch, du Sauhund, du Dreck, Hände hoch, gnädige Frau, Hände hoch Sie wünschen, Hände hoch zweimal Kaffee bitte.* Wait for me, I shouted. I scrambled up to the windowsill, jumped out of the window, and ran after him. I'm right behind you, wait for me. I don't know if he heard my scream or if he was deafened by the shrill whistle because immediately after I shouted he fell, and I ran on until the whistle and pain deafened me as well, until a warm wave came over me and covered me in darkness. . . .

So I should thank fate that now, from a distance of

twenty meters, I can look through a pane of glass at his face, alive, smiling. So what if it's a woman's? She's getting impatient; she glances toward the door. It's already ten after eight. I should have arrived by now, sat down at the dainty table, on the green plush, in front of a dainty slice of cake. This is Henryk's wife. You know, Henryk my brother, the one who didn't want to go with us.

No, she won't say that in front of me. But she's said it many times, in many places: He stayed because of her. He didn't want to escape with us, Mother begged him, but he didn't want to leave her. After the war she wrote one postcard: The Germans shot Henryk in '43. Mother fainted. We kept on sending her letters but she never answered.

Their letters said: We don't understand why there's no word from you. Then: *I* don't understand why there's no word from you. (Apparently his mother was no longer alive.) We have a right, *I* have a right to know the details, I want to know.

I had torn up the letters. Their words were engraved on my memory, including those last ones, blatantly cruel: He died because of you. They were there in every letter, even if you couldn't see them on the paper. They were there; they are there now and will be there later and would be there even if neither Henryk's sister nor her letters ever existed.

This is Henryk's wife, my brother who was killed. What would you like to drink? Coffee? Dear, please be so kind as to ask. . . . They will judge me with polite smiles. They will look at my hand, deformed by the bullet that failed to hit me in the heart as I ran after him. They'll guess the location of the second scar, the bullet that hit my hip, from the way I walk, my limp.

. . . When I regained consciousness everything was quiet: a fly was sitting on my face; the door to our house was wide open. As I lay there, weak, under the clear July sky, my first conscious thought was: Henryk will be right back. I waited for him a long time, warding off the waves of warmth and darkness that kept washing over me. Only when the sun shone on my face did I manage to turn my head a little. I saw him—foreshortened, from an angle that the most skilled photographer would have been proud of, his huge legs thrown apart, the bare soles pointing upward, and then, and then . . .

They're anxious. The plump hand pulling back a cuff, a glance at a watch. A cigarette. They're waiting. A compact in Henryk's hand, his head inclined toward a mirror, powder patted onto his nose. She's beautiful.

. . . with great effort, groaning, I crawled over to him. I already knew everything there was to know: the two flies on the big toe of his right foot had not escaped my notice. They made me understand, destroyed my hope. The grass beneath me grew damp. Trailing my useless leg behind me, I called his name. He was unreachable now and far away. I dragged myself the last short distance to him, screaming. He had no face. . . .

Pry your hands off the green fence, straighten your fingers, take a deep breath. The wind coming off the lake is so cold!

He had no face.

They're getting up, there's not much time left, take a good look, take it with you, memorize it. She's buttoning her jacket, she's scanning the room, she's pouting. Why did she laugh before? She shouldn't have laughed! All I have to do is get out of their way, take a few steps back; that's all.

They're coming out. She walks gracefully.

"Maybe she'll call again. I can't understand it." She squints at the lake. Does she expect me to emerge from the water? The plump man takes her arm.

Call her name! Then you can look at Henryk's face as long as you want. My throat is dry. *Click, click,* her heels along the sidewalk, the saberlike umbrella hanging by her side. . . .

He had no face.

I can't catch up with them now. Even if I crawl as I did then, I won't see his face. The man raises his hand, hails a taxi. They're gone.

My hotel is on the riverfront, a narrow building with several stories. The porter hands me the key and asks if he should wake me in the morning.

"Nein, danke," I answer.

In the room I switch on the lamp, sit down on the bed. I take out the sleeping powder I purchased in the drugstore and wash it down with a glass of lukewarm water from the tap. As I wait for sleep I try to remember what Henryk's face looked like. But once again he has no face.

CHEERFUL ZOFIA

She says things are all right now because she's gone through ther-a-py, and the doctor, who was very good, helped her.

She is cheerful, she lives in a cheerful room, she fixed it up herself, she sewed the curtains herself from muslin, she embroidered the tablecloth herself, herself, herself—because who else was there? She is com-plete-ly a-lone.

She pronounces certain phrases in a singsong rhythm, pausing between syllables; it's unclear if she's trying to emphasize their meaning or if she speaks that way because of what happened to her. She lived in the Children's Home for many years; now she lives on her own and works in a clothing factory. She likes to sew. You don't have to talk when you're sewing, she says, laughing. It's not that talking is difficult for her. The ther-a-py helped her a lot, but still . . . she hesitates . . . she doesn't really like to talk. She went for so long without talking that silence became a habit.

She checks carefully to see if I've understood her.

"Habit is a second nature," she explains.

She has the smooth face of a child and a thin, fragile body.

"Back then when they found me I was like a little monkey. A mon-key. Part human, part animal. My hands were long and thin; my hair came down to my waist; my body was covered with scabs. This is how I talked . . ." She laughs, and gestures with her hands.

"They asked me who I was and I did this . . ." She shrugs her shoulders, spreads her hands. "And when they asked me what my name was, I did this . . ." Again she shrugs. "I was in the courtyard, squatting on my haunches, the children kept pointing at me, calling me mon-key. But the older ones said, 'A mute. A Jewish mute.' "

She pours some more tea.

"Do you understand?" She checks once again, then slides a piece of cake toward me—cake she has baked herself. She likes to cook, to bake.

"In the factory they call me cheerful Zofia."

Why? Well, because she's cheerful and likes to laugh, just like that, at the slightest provocation. In her case, everything expresses itself as cheerfulness. Others are sad and melancholy after what they went through. But not her—and it's strange. She heard the doctor say that this was a symp-tom.

She smoothes out the tablecloth she embroidered with bright colors and laughs nervously when I ask her to tell me something else about her experiences.

"What's there to say? I was in that barn for two winters." She counts them out. "That means I came in the autumn, then there was the first winter, then spring, summer, the second autumn, the second winter, and then a little bit of the second spring.

"Those last two months I stayed there only because I didn't know that the war was over. And if the peasants hadn't come to tear down that barn, which was standing there at the edge of the forest, empty and abandoned, who knows how long I would have stayed there." She thinks for a moment and adds, "Probably not long, because the doctor says I would have died."

No one ever entered the barn—just some children once or twice, but they didn't climb up under the roof where she was hiding. She lay along the rafter that supported the ceiling, and at night she would slide down the post to get roots. She also stole beets and potatoes. She remembers one lucky day when she found an empty can.

"Do you know what I made out of that can?" She bursts out laughing. "I made a chamber pot out of it. I would cover it with a stone."

And the second one she found was for water.

"When I had water in the can, a pile of roots, and potatoes, then I was calm. I lay there quietly, sometimes I gnawed on a root, sometimes on a bit of potato . . . I washed it down with water. . . ."

But all that time she never used her voice.

"And what else?" She mulls it over, searching. "I don't know, myself. . . ." Finally she says, "What I remember best is the silence. But you can't talk about silence. Silence is the opposite of talk," she explains.

I ask about her life before the war.

She doesn't know where she was born. She doesn't know who her parents were. She has forgotten everything. Nor does she remember how she came to be in the forest, but she does remember that she wandered in the forest for a very long time before she hid in the old barn.

Suddenly animated, she says, "After the war they drove me around the neighboring villages where Jews once lived; they even took me to a town. They put me on display, like in a circus. 'Whose is she?' they asked. There weren't any Jews in the villages, and only four left in the town. They didn't know who I was. And there was nothing that could be done. And that's how it would have to be.

"I chose a name for myself. Zofia. It's nice, isn't it? I liked it right away."

I don't ask any more questions, but Zofia is thinking about something and for the first time seems to be concentrating. And now she really does resemble a helpless little monkey.

She says, "Other people suffered so much. . . . But no one beat or tortured me. . . . I never saw a German. . . . But still it's as if they killed me. Because I'm not the same person. My name, my date of birth—they're not mine. The doctor said it's shock. I don't know what happened before then, or what I was like. So it's as if I didn't exist."

Tiny drops of moisture bead up on her forehead. She wipes them off with the back of her hand and with this gesture seems to wipe away the thoughts that torment her, because once again she smiles and says, "Did you ever see someone who was killed in the war but who is still alive?"

BIRDS

No sooner had they taken their seats than the little boy asked for a roll.

"He adores eating on the train." Darling laughed. When Darling laughed everything about her laughed: her gleaming white teeth, her eyes—not quite brown, nor quite green—and the dimples in her cheeks, which everyone considered the main source of all her charm. Darling was a charming young woman, which was why she was nicknamed Darling. Her real name—Jozefina—seemed a little too grand, too formal.

"He just ate breakfast an hour ago," the man pointed out.

"It's one thing to eat at home, and another to eat on the train," she explained. "All children adore eating on trains. I'm sure you did as well. . . ." And she gave the boy a ham sandwich she had fixed for the trip, wrapped in fresh waxed paper, very appetizing.

The man wanted to say, Please stop saying "adore," every other sentence, I can't stand words like that, but instead he said, "It's so hot. . . ."

Darling's teeth, dimples, and eyes were all laughing. "What do you mean, 'hot'? Just a second ago I was thinking we should have packed more sweaters. The radio says there's going to be a cold snap. But no rain." She was in a good mood; she wanted nothing to do with clouds, not even in the sky.

They were going on vacation. Darling had picked the place and finally told him a week ago: it was a quiet hideaway surrounded by woods, in the middle of nowhere. "You should be able to get some work done there."

At first he hadn't realized where that middle of nowhere was. Only when she had begun to explain how to get there did he interrupt her, and, scarcely changing his tone of voice, he asked if it wouldn't be better to go to some other place, not quite so remote: to the mountains, perhaps, or the lakes. She disagreed strongly and reminded him how much he complained about the hordes of acquaintances who would immediately descend on them like flies. Like flies! You like flies? I want to relax, you have to write, why do we need flies? We have them all year, as it is.

"Besides," she'd confessed, "I've already rented the place. It's wonderful; it has a garden overlooking the river. It's cheap. It's perfect."

She hadn't registered the silence with which he greeted her enthusiasm. She was bustling around the room; he was standing by the window. He lit his pipe and puffed on it nervously. When he turned around a moment later and began, "You know what, Joziu . . . ?" (he only used her real name at critical moments), he noticed that his wife had left the room. He heard water running in the bathroom; she was taking a shower.

Maybe it's better this way, he thought, and the subject was dropped.

Darling was his second wife, his wife from after the war, very young. He loved her, and they had a three-year-old son.

The train pulled out on time, at ten o'clock. It was probably the same train as back then; after all, there weren't any other connections, except perhaps a night train, which was impossible because of the child. Besides, it would have troubled him more to steal past that place at night, under cover of darkness. The day itself was sunny, just like back then, except back then it was early spring. The fragrant forest . . . a flock of birds . . .

"The rain was coming down in sheets, back then," Lina's parents' neighbor had said.

So there were two "then's" and today's "now," which in a few hours would become another "then." Right now this third "then" seemed the hardest, since the first one could only be imagined, which he was incapable of doing, or else he refused to try. And he had experienced the second "then" by himself. But now there were three of them traveling, and that was what was unbearable; that they were going on vacation, going to a house overlooking the river, happy and cheerful, and that all three would pass by in full view of the others. In full view of the others, he thought, and was horrified by his choice of words. I should never have come with them. Darling should have gone on with the child, and he should have followed, alone. Why hadn't he thought of that earlier? Nonsense, he told himself. Nonsense, nonsense, he repeated in his mind. It didn't help.

"I keep looking at you and looking at you, and I know all you're thinking about is Karolina."

He shuddered like someone roused from a dream and nearly asked who Karolina was—which certainly would have upset Darling. Karolina was the heroine of the novel he had been working on for well over a year. Lately it had been very difficult for him to write. He was stuck; he had no energy. Darling pinned great hopes on this retreat to the woods, far from bothersome flies.

"I've had enough of her." He smiled awkwardly. "I'll probably lock her up in some drawer."

"What? Are you giving up that easily?" She was indignant. She looked at him carefully. She had noticed that he was not his usual self lately, and she attributed this to the daily defeats he suffered at his desk. She wanted to go on discussing his problems with his novel, but even though everything she said always made a good deal of sense, he always managed to change the subject. Now he said he had a headache; he didn't want to think about Karolina now. And he almost made another mistake when Darling, obediently changing the subject, asked him when they were going to arrive. In two hours, he almost said, which was absurd; that was how long it would take them to reach Lina's hometown, where she had lived before they were married and then again after he had enlisted and she returned to her parents. It would take five hours before they would get to their isolated country retreat. An awfully long journey.

He burrowed into the corner, closed his eyes, and escaped into a kind of half sleep. The sunlight fell directly on his face, gentle and kind. Darling was talking to the boy in a hushed voice about cows and trees. Then the waxed paper rustled; she gave the child another sandwich, then more rustling. He peeked out from under his eyelids. Darling, too, was eating a roll.

He watched her in secret, with a distaste he had never felt before, with the cold eyes of a stranger. She chewed slowly, like a child, and just like a child eating something delicious, she let her eyelids droop while she savored her food. Her face is ordinary, he thought, knowing that this was untrue and that he was wronging her, not only because he was judging her but because of the way he was looking at her.

"What does the wind smell like?" she was asking the boy.

"It smells like wind."

"Not true, the wind smells like clover," she said, laughing. They were like two children.

He must have dozed off, because suddenly the sun was no longer shining on his face, and fluffy white clouds were drifting across the sky.

He began to worry whether the bridge, a permanently temporary bridge, as Lina's parents' neighbor had said, came right before the town or quite a bit earlier. Just after crossing the bridge, the tracks climb uphill, and for about two kilometers the train crawls slowly along the steep embankment, bordered on both sides by forest.

"It was the best place for jumping," the neighbor had said. "Look around, nothing but trees, and every train, even *that* one, had to slow down whether it wanted to or not. This is where they jumped."

The neighbor led him down the embankment to the edge of the forest. They startled a flock of birds, which swooped off their branches and took off soaring into the sky.

The oaks were old, spreading. The neighbor said, "Right here," and pointed at a tree near where the road led into the forest. There, beneath that old oak, Lina and his little son had lain murdered. He had bent over, plucked a blade of grass, and put it in his uniform pocket.

That was in 1945; he hadn't been demobilized yet. He and the neighbor went back the way they had come, on foot, and the neighbor told him what he knew. He listened in silence, and when they reached the station, he thanked him, bade him farewell, climbed aboard the train, and left.

The child was cranky; Darling was holding him on her lap.

In the only photograph he still had left, Lina is holding a baby on her knees. The child's face is mushy, unclear, featureless. Lina is looking into the camera, serious, lost in thought. He had shown Darling that photo before they were married.

"She's beautiful. But why was she so sad?"

"She wasn't sad, but she wasn't very cheerful either," he said.

He couldn't explain what she was really like, and he didn't want to say, She was different than you.

He touched Darling's cheek. "My love . . ." He wasn't sure whether he was speaking to her or to Lina. Or maybe to both of them? Once he loved that woman. Now he loved this one.

He looked at his watch, took out his pipe and filled it, stood up, gestured with his pipe that he wanted to smoke, and went into the corridor. He shut the compartment door behind him, separating himself from the two of them.

The train was still moving fast. He stood there and waited. Suddenly the rhythm of the wheels changed. He leaned out and caught sight of the permanently temporary wooden bridge. Slowly but surely, both the bridge and the dense, leafy forest were coming closer and closer. Tall weeds at the bottom of the ravine. And, above the forest, birds.

The locomotive whistled shrilly, like a bird.

"We used to listen for it in town, and when we heard that whistle, we all knew the train had reached the bridge and that, as soon as they crossed over it, people would try to escape. . . ."

Clickety-clack, clickety-clack, slower and slower, like a heartbeat wearing out. The groan of the spans. The steep banks of gravel tumbling down toward the woods.

They stood on the roofs with their rifles and fired away as if they were shooting birds. . . . He saw people jumping, flying out of the train like birds, soaring, fluttering, crashing down to the ground, dead, and the knowledge that they had been transformed into birds comforted him, a little.

He looked for the spot where the road led into the forest. He found it. "Right here."

Parked by the road was a little passenger car, and beside it, under a spreading oak tree, a family with children sat around a folding table, having dinner. The children jumped up, raced over the embankment, waved their little hands wildly, and shouted something in their high-pitched voices. Without thinking he raised his hand to return their greeting.

The boy was sleeping. Darling was reading a book: her glasses made her look endearingly comical.

"Already?"

"Already what?" he asked anxiously.

"You've already finished your pipe?" she asked, smiling.

He stroked her hair. She smiled again, still reading.

I'll tell her . . . I'll tell her tonight, he thought, suddenly filled with tenderness and peace.

TRACES

CHARACTERS

WOMAN I, twenty-two years old
VILLAGE ELDER, sixty-five years old
WOMAN II, forty years old
DOCTOR, sixty years old
FISHERMAN, fifty years old
BOY, stutters, eighteen years old, known as the village idiot
HUSBAND OF WOMAN II, forty-five years old

I

WOMAN I: It was sometime in 1942. Sometime in the spring, probably March or April . . . After all, you're the one who—

ELDER: But I keep telling you, madam, I just don't know. I never saw her, never even heard of her. People said somebody was hiding at the Kempinskis', but those were just rumors. And nobody ever asked old Kempinski about it, because . . . well, you understand. Besides, he was a pretty nasty guy and, well, not very approachable. The wife was all right. But he put the fear of God in her; she wouldn't say a word without making sure it was fine with him; she wouldn't take a step; she was always at his beck and call. But it's true that people said they were hiding somebody. Kempinski was quite a gardener. They had a beautiful vegetable garden.

WOMAN I: And you never heard the name Stanislava Pokolska?

ELDER: I didn't say that. I know the name, and once I even saw her. But that couldn't have been your sister. This woman was sixty-five years old; she was staying at the doctor's; she said she was some kind of relative. I knew Stanislava Pokolska, all right, but I didn't know your sister. The Stanislava Pokolska I knew was an older woman; she came here to spend her vacation at the doctor's. She was heavy, with glasses.

WOMAN I: I know my sister was at the Kempinskis'; I'm absolutely sure of it. I also know she had papers made out to Stanislava Pokolska. And as I told you, my sister was twelve years old at the time. Maybe the papers belonged to Pani Pokolska's daughter, or rather her granddaughter.

ELDER: Maybe. Why don't you ask the doctor? But why did she need papers if she was hiding? Nobody ever saw her.

WOMAN 1: I don't know. Maybe someone did see her. I've been inside the house just for a minute, but long enough to see some letters carved in the windowsill with a pocketknife: *S.P.* and next to that *M.* My sister's real name was Mila; I mean it was really Emilia, but we called her Mila.

ELDER: You mean they let you in?

WOMAN 1: Who? The new owners? They let me in. But they weren't exactly thrilled about it.

ELDER: They're relatives of Kempinski, and even more unpleasant than he was. The kind of city people who look down their noses at country folk. Because they're from the city. He's a bookkeeper; every day he goes into town to work. They've let the garden go so badly it's terrible. If Kempinski were alive, he'd pull his hair out—or else he'd take a cane to them. Because you have to realize, madam, he was a real hothead. It wasn't a very nice family.

WOMAN 1: Hothead?

ELDER: That's what I said. If he hadn't been such a hothead he'd still be around today. He had a fight with his wife and rushed off to his boat. I'm sure you noticed there's a lake behind their house. His wife ran after him and jumped into the boat; they rowed out to the middle of the lake. They kept yelling at each other in the boat, so loudly people could hear them. And then suddenly a storm blew up. . . . But that doesn't have anything to do with your sister.

WOMAN 1: No. I wrote to them right after the war and heard back from the local records office that neither was alive. Maybe if I had been able to come . . . if I hadn't been sick for so long. I've only been back in the country a week—I came straight here.

ELDER: You did the right thing. You have to convince yourself that you've done everything you could.

WOMAN 1: Everything. Right. But what does that mean, "everything"? You were the elder back then. I thought you might be able to help me. I thought you would know something.

ELDER: Stanislava Pokolska. She was registered here on a temporary permit. But I've already told you; she was an older woman. She stayed here for a month or two; she often went away, God knows where. The village is very spread out; the doctor lives at the other end. And besides, who asked about things like that? People were glad to be alive, in one piece, just to be left alone. . . .

WOMAN 1: Even so, people were saying that Kempinski was hiding someone. What people? Maybe you remember who told you.

ELDER: Stach Wiernik told me. But you won't get very far looking for him. He died in Auschwitz. They took him away in 1941, and he never came back.

WOMAN 1: My sister was still at home in 1941. This Stach Wiernik couldn't have been talking about her. He must have been talking about someone else.

ELDER: I don't know who he was talking about. He just said in a general way that Kempinski was quite a guy. So I asked him why. And then he told me he had heard that Kempinski was hiding someone.

WOMAN I: That means he wasn't hiding just my sister.

ELDER: Looks that way. Once the Germans came and turned the place upside down. But they didn't find anyone.

WOMAN I: When was that?

ELDER: Later. In 1942 or 1943. Two officers and a man in civilian clothes. But they didn't find anybody.

WOMAN I: Are you sure?

ELDER: Of course I'm sure.

WOMAN I: But that's when my sister was staying at Kempinski's.

ELDER: If she was, they would have found her.

WOMAN I: She might have had a hideout. . . . I'm going to go there one more time. I'll ask that woman if she'll let me look around. Maybe I'll find some trace.

ELDER: Good idea. Look for a trace. The first clue often leads to a second, the second to the third, and so on. . . .

WOMAN I: Thank you. Sorry for bothering you. I may come back later.

ELDER: Please feel free. But I can't help you; I don't know anything.

WOMAN 1: I know. But there's always . . . I don't know . . . maybe there's something I forgot to ask. Maybe . . .

ELDER: Now let me ask you something. Why are you doing this? Your sister didn't come back. The war's been over for almost two years. That means she didn't make it.

WOMAN 1: Maybe she's still alive and looking for me. She didn't know where I was, or what happened to me, but I knew that she was at the Kempinskis'. Nobody from my family survived. The neighborhood where we used to live is in ruins. If only I'd come back right after the war. But I couldn't. After the camp I was very sick. I had spinal tuberculosis.

ELDER: But even then you wouldn't have found out any more. Nobody here ever heard of her. Unless the doctor knows something . . .

WOMAN 1: I'll go back to the Kempinskis' house, then I'll look up the doctor.

ELDER: Well. Good luck.

WOMAN 1: Thank you.

2

WOMAN I: It's me again. Please forgive me for bothering you.

WOMAN II: It's no bother. I just don't understand. There's nothing I can tell you. We've only been here a year. Before that I never set foot in this house, and I only knew the Kempinskis in passing. To tell the truth, I only saw them once, and that was at my wedding. Kempinski was my husband's uncle. That's all.

WOMAN I: I was wondering. . . . Could I look around some more?

WOMAN II: Look around? Why? Do you think that . . . no, I never, that's too . . . I don't know what to say.

WOMAN I: I'd simply like to look around—at the attic and the cellar. Maybe I'll find some kind of trace.

WOMAN II: You're a little strange, you know. But go ahead and look. Hurry, though. Before my husband gets back. He wouldn't like it. Besides, there isn't any cellar. Have you ever seen a house without a cellar? How could they have lived here? There's just a little root cellar, and now that's overflowing with potatoes. We've already stocked up for the winter.

WOMAN I: Thank you. I'll try to be as quick as I can.

WOMAN II: What are you staring at?

WOMAN I: This morning, when I was here, I found some letters carved into the windowsill with a penknife. Here, look: *S.P.* My sister's papers were made out to Stanislava Pokolska. And here, the letter *M.* My sister's real name was Mila. That's a trace.

WOMAN II: What do you mean? Anyway, you already know she was here. So that trace doesn't really mean much. I thought you were trying to find out what happened to your sister after she left this house.

WOMAN I: After she left? How do you know she ever left this house?

WOMAN II: Maybe they took her somewhere else. Who knows . . . a lot of things could have happened. And the elder, what did he say? Didn't he know anything?

WOMAN I: He heard that the Kempinskis were hiding someone in 1941—before they took in my sister. And even more important, he also knew someone named Stanislava Pokolska, an older woman, a relative of the doctor. But because the doctor lives at the other end of the village, I decided to stop by here first. So would it be all right if I looked around?

WOMAN II: Just make it quick, my husband . . . this was their living room. We didn't change anything; we don't have the money to buy new furniture. Everything is the way it was. It's all so horribly ugly.

WOMAN I: Maybe I'll start with the attic. I saw the dormer from outside. (*Sound of steps on stairs.*) Oh, I see, it's not an attic, it's a little room, all fixed up and furnished.

WOMAN II: It's furnished, all right. We haven't changed a thing.

WOMAN I: Bed, wardrobe, table, dresser . . . obviously somebody was living here.

WOMAN II: It seems that way.

WOMAN I: Didn't your husband ever mention that his relatives were hiding someone?

WOMAN II: No. He wasn't close to them. Kempinski was a gardener. He worked like an ox his whole life, and then he came to a miserable end.

WOMAN I: I know. The elder told me. He and his wife both drowned in the lake during a storm.

WOMAN II: Exactly. We inherited the house and the garden. If it weren't for that, we'd still be living in town. I couldn't be sorrier. I don't like the country.

WOMAN I: Would you mind if I opened the dresser drawer?

WOMAN II: Go ahead and open it. Go ahead and look around, but make it quick.

WOMAN I: Here are some letters. No, they're just scraps of a letter that's been torn up.

WOMAN II: Maybe your sister wrote it?

WOMAN I: No . . . my sister was thirteen years old, and the handwriting here is more like an adult's. "Dear Mother,

Be sure to send my sweater, the old one with the green stripes, because it's cold at night, and if you could also . . ." Just scraps. ". . . water in the lake is blue as the sky . . . springtime . . . please send . . ."

WOMAN II: Who knows. You can't even tell whether it was a man or a woman writing. But whoever wrote it was right. A heavy chill rolls in off the lake at night. Except that the water is green, not blue. What else does it say?

WOMAN I: I can't read it; the ink is all smeared.

WOMAN II: That's the moisture from the lake. You can feel it in your bones. And my husband wanted to live in the country! If only the air did him good—but there's no chance of that! Your ears ache, your knees ache. . . . What's all that stuff?

WOMAN I: A candle stub, a bandage, a purse—empty. Wait a minute, here's another little scrap . . . this handwriting's different; it's tiny. Someone else wrote this. "The thing we feared would happen has happened . . . this morning . . . suddenly . . ."

WOMAN II: Suddenly what? What's wrong?

WOMAN I: "The thing we feared would happen has happened . . ." That might have some connection with my sister. The pieces must fit together somehow. "The thing we feared would happen . . ." Just a minute.

WOMAN II: Do you think your sister wrote that?

WOMAN I: No. That's not a young girl's handwriting, but who knows. She didn't have anyone to write to . . . maybe she kept a diary, for all I know. Everything's torn to shreds. "One shirt and a pair of leather pumps, too."

WOMAN II: Leather pumps!

WOMAN I: ". . . have to wipe out every trace . . . I shall always . . ."

WOMAN II: "Wipe out every trace"! And traces are just what you're looking for.

WOMAN I: "I kiss you as tenderly as I can, my love. . . ." It's a love letter.

WOMAN II: She might have fallen in love. Twelve, thirteen years old—that's old enough to fall in love.

WOMAN I: That's all I can make out. The writing's completely illegible, and the letter was torn up so deliberately. Oh, you see—"I love . . . take care . . . children. . . ." It must mean "take care of the children."

WOMAN II: A husband writing to his wife. A married couple with children. The Kempinskis didn't have any children.

WOMAN I: Just a second, just a second—there's something else.

WOMAN II: You've got good eyes!

WOMAN I: It's not a letter; it's a receipt. "I hereby acknowledge the receipt of three jars of marmalade and ten eggs." Evidently some kind of code . . .

WOMAN II: Partisans, maybe. There were plenty of partisans in the woods around here.

WOMAN I: I didn't think of that. How could I not have? Of course—she might have escaped to the woods; maybe they took her to the woods. She didn't look Jewish; she had long blond braids, blue eyes. I have to find out.

WOMAN II: From whom? Without a name, without an address . . .

WOMAN I: I'm going to keep searching. I'm sure the elder will know something.

3

ELDER: And what about that Pokolska woman? What did the doctor tell you?

WOMAN I: I haven't been to see the doctor yet. I was at the Kempinskis'. You know, there were partisans hiding out at the Kempinskis'. . . .

ELDER: I thought you were looking for your sister.

WOMAN I: I am. But think a minute: my sister was at the Kempinskis'; I know that for a fact. Now I also know that people from the underground were hiding there: I found some scraps of letters and a coded receipt. Listen: "I hereby acknowledge the receipt of three jars of marmalade and ten eggs." That's some kind of code, I'm sure.

ELDER: And what if it is?

WOMAN I: Maybe she took to the woods with the partisans? Wiernik must have said something about partisans.

ELDER: There weren't any partisans around here in '41.

WOMAN I: But later. She might have gone with them later? You understand . . .

ELDER: Maybe, but not necessarily . . .

WOMAN I: Please, tell me who in the village fought with the partisans.

ELDER: Different people.

WOMAN I: Who?

ELDER: You want names? That's something else again. There were different outfits, and right now the one that was active around here isn't a big favorite with the government. So I can't give you any names, and besides I don't want to. After what people around here went through, they just want to be left alone.

WOMAN I: I went through enough myself.

ELDER: I can imagine. . . . Well, how was the bookkeeper's wife—was she annoyed?

WOMAN I: No. She was actually quite nice. But trust me a little, I beg you. Please—I won't tell a living soul.

ELDER: I can't, madam. And to tell the truth, I myself don't even know who and what and how. In any case, I doubt whether your sister would have gone into the woods with them, or that they would have taken her. Not only was she Jewish, she was too young. Thirteen-year-olds like that were just a nuisance. Did you find anything else?

WOMAN I: A few more scraps of letters. In one of them somebody wrote that the thing they feared would happen happened. Maybe somebody informed the Germans that the Kempinskis were hiding a Jewish girl? You said something about a raid.

ELDER: They didn't find anybody then. We don't even know who or what they were looking for.

WOMAN I: Kempinski must have been a brave man.

ELDER: He had a temper worse than the devil himself! But what a gardener! If you saw his cabbage. Heads like the domes of an Orthodox church. And his snapdragons—they were this big! He talked to his flowers. Why not? People talk to animals, why not to flowers?

4

DOCTOR: As a matter of fact, I can provide you with some information. My distant cousin Stanislava Pokolska kept pretty close ties with Kempinski. Incidentally, the Kempinskis were very nice people, although he was unusually highstrung, neurotic, and prone to bouts of depression. I assume you are familiar with the circumstances of their tragic death. A very sad accident and very . . . well . . . but to get back to the matter that concerns you. In April of 1942 Stanislava Pokolska provided Kempinski with documents belonging to her niece of the same name. At that time the girl was fourteen years old and was staying in a hostel run by Ursuline nuns somewhere outside of Warsaw. I know about it because Stanislava asked me whether she was endangering her niece. One evening, after she came back from the Kempinskis—she befriended them very quickly, which was unusual, since they were extremely reclusive—she told me about Kempinski's request and explained that he was going to bring a young girl in from Warsaw and would need the documents just for the length of the trip.

WOMAN I: Just for the length of the trip?

DOCTOR: Yes. I remember exactly: it was to protect her during the train ride. Stanislava gave him the documents—she traveled to the hostel to fetch them—and later he returned them.

WOMAN I: And my sister?

DOCTOR: I have no idea what became of her. Kempinski never mentioned her to me. I know that he brought her here in the spring of '42, when Stanislava was living with me for a few months. And that's all. . . . Wait, just a minute. Once Stanislava told me she had seen the little girl. One day at dusk she went over to take back a book or borrow a new one, and the door between the living room and the kitchen was open. Inside the room was a little girl sitting at a table. I remember that Stanislava was a little disturbed by Kempinski's reaction: he jumped up as if the house were on fire, slammed the door shut, and yelled at her, "Why didn't you knock? Whoever heard of someone walking right in without knocking?" Stanislava was—how should I say?—upset by his behavior; after all, why make such a fuss, since she was the one who had provided him with the documents, right? But she must have mentioned it to him again later, because when I asked her whether the Kempinskis still had that girl living with them, she told me, "Kempinski says they don't."

WOMAN I: Would you be so kind as to give me Pani Pokolska's address?

DOCTOR: But my dear . . . Stanislava Pokolska is no longer alive. She died just before the Warsaw Uprising.

WOMAN I: And her niece?

DOCTOR: I don't know anything about her; I never even saw her. And besides, what could she tell you? She probably didn't know anything about it. . . .

WOMAN I: So I don't know any more than I did before. She was here—and nobody knows what happened to her.

DOCTOR: Here, let me give you the address of a man who lives across the lake, in Polana. He's a fisherman as well as a ferryman, and he knew Kempinski pretty well. Maybe he'll know something. Tell him the doctor sent you.

5

FISHERMAN: Hmm ... that's ancient history. Old Kempinski—bless his soul, he was a restless sort. People thought all he cared about was mulching roses or planting cabbage. Little did they know. . . . But not even I suspected he was hiding a Jewish girl. He said that his brother-in-law's daughter had come for a week to get fattened up, since there was nothing to eat in town. . . . By the way, how did you—or your parents—get hooked up with Kempinski in the first place? Because he didn't have anybody in Warsaw, and rarely went there.

WOMAN 1: I don't know. I was seventeen years old at the time; my parents never talked to me about it. I never even saw the man. The first time I heard his name was in the fall of 1942, when they deported us to the camp, and my father said to me, "You're young; you might survive. Remember, once the war is over go to Polana Dolna, to Jozef Kempinski. Mila is there with him."

FISHERMAN: Well . . . I know he brought a child from Warsaw. Thin, with braids. She sat there in the boat like a block of wood. I didn't get a good look at her, and besides it was already dark outside. Kempinski said he was going to have to fatten her up a bit and grumbled about its being a lot of trouble for his wife, since she wasn't used to children. I took them in the boat from Polanka Gorna to Polana Dolna; after all, they lived right on the lake, on the other side.

WOMAN I: And what happened to her? Did you ever see her again?

FISHERMAN: If she was Jewish, they wouldn't exactly have kept her on display. I never saw her. But the next time I took Kempinski in the boat—ten days or maybe two weeks later—I asked him whether his niece had put on any weight. "What niece?" he asked. "You know, the one I brought over in the boat with you, Joziu . . . the other night. . . ." "Aah, Stasia." He laughed and said that she'd already gone back home and that she'd put on four pounds eating his wife's noodles. I didn't catch on then . . . old Kempinski managed to pull the wool over my eyes. . . .

WOMAN I: The Kempinskis died in 1944, a few months before liberation.

FISHERMAN: It was April 2, not a cloud in the sky that morning, and that afternoon a sudden storm came up . . .

WOMAN I: And my sister? She was still there. *Was.* Where is she now?

FISHERMAN: What are you asking? Don't you know what was going on then?

WOMAN I: I know that Kempinski had contacts with the partisans. . . .

FISHERMAN: With the partisans? I don't know about that.

WOMAN I: The elder told me.

FISHERMAN: What does he know? He and Kempinski were always at each other's throat. The elder would have drowned Kempinski in a spoon of water if he'd had the chance.

WOMAN I: I was in the house. I found a receipt made out by someone in the underground.

FISHERMAN: Old Kempinski—bless his soul—he was a restless sort. But as far as people went, he kept his mouth shut. Didn't even confess to the priest.

6

BOY: Miss! Miss! I heard what you were talking about with the fisherman. I was milking the cow in the stall and I heard you. I know. I saw her.

WOMAN I: Who are you? Whom did you see?

BOY: That girl . . . the one you were asking about. I know . . . I saw her. . . .

WOMAN I: When? My God . . . who are you?

BOY: I'm Jasio. Everybody says I'm dumb, but I saw her, that girl . . . the one you and the fisherman—

WOMAN I: You saw my sister? You know what happened to her?

BOY: I saw her. On Sunday. It was very hot. I went swimming in the lake. She was standing in the window.

WOMAN I: Where? What window?

BOY: At the Kempinskis', of course. In the attic.

WOMAN I: When did you see her? Please, tell me. My God . . . when was it?

BOY: The Hitler time. She was in the window. On Sunday. It was very hot. I went down to the lake. I walked through Kempinski's garden, that was the shortest way, it was hot, I wanted to cool off. On Sunday. She was behind the windowpane, in the window. The window was closed.

WOMAN I: And then what happened?

BOY: And then I called out to her, "Who are you?" And then Pani Kempinska came running out and took me by the hand into the house and asked, "Who are you talking to, Jasio?" "That girl in the window, Pani Kempinska." "You must have been seeing things; there's no girl there." "What do you mean, Pani Kempinska? I saw her myself." "Look," and she dragged me upstairs. The attic was empty—nobody in the window. I thought maybe the sun had made me see things, since it was so hot. That was on Sunday. Kempinski came and didn't say anything. He just looked at me like—

WOMAN I: Like how?

BOY: Like nothing. He just looked at me. . . . But he did give me a whipping. He beat me as hard as he could.

WOMAN I: Why did he beat you?

BOY: Not then, later.

WOMAN I: Why?

BOY: Because he thought I told the Germans he was hiding Jews.

WOMAN I: You informed the Germans?

BOY: I didn't inform any Germans. I swear I didn't. Ignac Burecki informed them. He was in with the Germans; he ran a kiosk at the station. He sold cigarettes, beer. He said to me, "You're an idiot, all right, Jasio, but you've got a head on your shoulders." When the Germans ran away, he packed up and ran with them. That's right.

WOMAN I: And how did this Burecki find out that somebody was hiding at the Kempinskis'? Did you tell him?

BOY: I guess so. It just slipped out. Because I saw her one more time, in the window. At night. I used to go there just to see if Mrs. Kempinska was pulling my leg. I'd sit in the bushes and look up at the window. Until one night—just by chance the moon was full—the window suddenly opened, and there she was, the same girl. . . . You know . . . I really liked her—that girl—from the first time. . . . I didn't think any bad thoughts, though. Oh no. The window suddenly opened, and she was standing in the window, her hair let down, her face as white as a saint's on a medallion.

WOMAN I: And what did you . . . ?

BOY: Nothing. She stood there for a while, then closed the window. I wanted to call up to her, but it was too late. I sat in the bushes all night long. I really liked her.

WOMAN I: So much that you informed Pan Burecki.

BOY: I didn't inform. I swear I didn't. It just slipped out. I didn't even say she was Jewish. It was Burecki who said "They're hiding a Jewish girl" and sent in the Germans. He was hungry for money, because back then they were paying money and vodka for any Jew sent their way. Not far from here there was a case where they paid five hundred zlotys and five liters of vodka for a textile merchant from the city.

WOMAN I: And the Germans took her away. . . .

BOY: What do you mean? They didn't find her. They searched the whole house. That's when Burecki threatened me, and Kempinski beat the daylights out of me. My ass was so sore that for two days I could barely sit.

WOMAN I: And what happened to her? Didn't you ever see her again? Please, tell me the truth. That was my sister.

BOY: I know, I heard you talking to the fisherman. I did see her again. At the station in Polana. She was sitting on the bench, waiting for the train.

WOMAN I: Waiting for the train? When . . . when? Are you sure you're not getting things confused?

BOY: Just after the Germans left, miss. Just after the war. She was sitting on the bench waiting for the train. I recognized her. She was sitting on the bench, with a scarf around her head and a basket beside her. She was waiting for the train, the one that comes at six in the evening. It stops in Polana for one minute. She was sitting on the bench, with a basket next to her. In her arms she was holding a baby.

WOMAN I: A *baby*?

BOY: I'm telling you: a baby.

WOMAN I: That couldn't be her.

BOY: It was her, the same one. I recognized her right away, even though she looked a little different. But it was her; I'd bet my life on it.

WOMAN I: With a *baby*?

BOY: That's right. A little baby. The baby was wrapped up in a little checked blanket. And she was in a coat and scarf. I looked at her very carefully.

WOMAN I: With a baby? Where did she get a baby?

BOY: Ha, ha . . . I'm sure you know that, miss. . . .

WOMAN 1: I meant, whose baby was it?

BOY: It was her baby. You could tell. The way she held it. The train came; she crossed herself, got on board, and rode away.

7

WOMAN 1: Doctor . . . I'm so upset. . . . You were the only doctor in the area. . . .

DOCTOR: Fourteen and a half years old . . . a rare case, I would have remembered it, and I don't. That Jasio, madam, he's a poor orphan. . . . Oh he's sly all right, but his imagination gets the better of him, the way it often does with handicapped people who want to call attention to themselves. If I were you I would take everything he says with a grain of salt.

WOMAN 1: But I sense that he's telling the truth.

DOCTOR: Of course. The fact that I didn't deliver the baby doesn't mean that your sister did *not* give birth. It's possible to give birth without a doctor—it happens.

8

WOMAN II: What a story! That means, according to what that idiot Jasio told you, you've found your sister . . . a living trace. Of course you can't rely on him. When somebody's known as the local idiot, it's probably not without reason. Maybe he was just imagining things.

WOMAN I: He described her—fair-skinned with long hair. That was her. . . . I came to have one last look at the attic.

WOMAN II: Do you think we're hiding something from you? Why are you crying?

WOMAN I: I just want to say good-bye.

WOMAN II: I don't understand. . . . To whom?

WOMAN I: Oh, I don't even understand myself. I want to say good-bye to my sister, and that's the only place where I'm sure she's been.

WOMAN II: Say good-bye? If she really survived, sooner or later you'll find her.

WOMAN I: No, I don't believe I will. Especially now that I've found out she did survive—I've lost all hope. So many announcements in the papers, on the radio, in different committees—and nothing. Absolute silence. It's very strange, but now that I've found a trace, I have the feeling that I'll never find her . . . that she's not looking for me . . . and that she never will. . . . That she doesn't want to find me.

WOMAN II: You know, I'm not cut out for this kind of thing; I'm more straightforward and simple, I don't think so roundabout. If she's alive, then she can be found. Except if I were you, I wouldn't listen to idiots. That's the truth.

WOMAN I: I'm going upstairs for a minute. The train leaves in half an hour. The same one she left on. At six P.M.

WOMAN II: The same one because there isn't any other. *(Sound of steps on stairs.)* Why don't you freshen up a bit; you've been crying so hard your face looks awful. . . . Oh dear, my husband will be here any minute. You're leaving just in time, I have to put the potatoes on.

9

WOMAN II: Did you know your uncle was hiding a Jewish girl?

HUSBAND: I didn't have the faintest idea. That's a strange story, all right. . . .

WOMAN II: Strange? That's a good one. As if there were only one or two people who disappeared, nobody knows when or where, without a trace? But she listened to what that idiot told her as if he were a prophet! What's the matter with you? Why aren't you eating?

HUSBAND: You know . . . I just remembered something. The first time I came out here after the accident . . . I just now remembered this little detail—I found a wooden cradle in front of the house. I thought it was very strange: my aunt and uncle didn't have any children, there weren't any grandchildren, and the house had been locked up and vacant for several months. That's right. I remember thinking how strange it was—of all things, a cradle—and I thought, Maybe someone's inside. I called out, "Hello? Anybody home?" Nobody answered. And, of course, there wasn't anybody there. I completely forgot about that. Where is she?

WOMAN II: She's already left for the station. It's six o'clock on the dot. The train will just be pulling away. . . .

10

Rumble of an approaching train. The train pulls up to the station, stops; the steam engine hisses. After a pause, a whistle, the signal to depart. The sound of wheels being turned by the pistons, slow at first, then faster and faster. At the same time sounds of steps running along the platform behind the train.

BOY: Miss! Miss! . . . I have to tell you something . . . something important . . . something very important . . .

(*The rumble of the train fades into silence.)*

JULIA

Julia had come for a vacation with her children and wound up staying on in our town. In September, her husband, Szymon, who was big and strong, with black whiskers, joined her, driven east by the invasion of Poland.

I remember Julia from the last days of August; how she floated through the dusty market, the wide brim of her black straw hat flapping like wings, Julia, still slender, wearing a sand-colored dress and sand-colored gloves that came up to her elbows. She was chic and sophisticated, with a graceful walk and shapely legs.

"It's amazing how some women are able to adapt," said Henio, the friend of her youth, who had come back to his homeland all the way from Paris and who, like Julia, wound up staying in our town. "The last time I saw her she was living with her husband in the country," he told me (as if I didn't know this) as he gazed after Julia, who was moving farther and farther away.

"They were living in a room they rented from a peasant couple. Julia worked in the fields with them; she adopted their way of cooking, their way of dress. She wore wide skirts and old sweaters and started saying things only a peasant would say. In the evening, while she was helping the wife feed the pigs, I would pass the time by reading Proust, who shared her bookshelf with a first-aid manual—the village didn't have a doctor. I was amazed by her metamorphosis. After all, I've known her since we were children. Proust on the shelf and Julia feeding pigs. And now, once again . . ." He turned his head, which was covered with wisps of thin hair; his eyes, as blue as forget-me-nots, expressed profound amazement as well as admiration.

It was early afternoon; the sun was broiling. Julia's latest incarnation was moving away with a light step, in a sand-colored dress and black straw wings. No one but her immediate family knew that she hadn't purchased the black and the sand, that she hadn't made any decisions about style or color; they were a gift from a rich relation. No one could have imagined this because Julia looked as if she had been dressing in Parisian sands and Florentine straw all her life. The farther she floated away, the more the sands merged with the colors of the dusty marketplace, and soon all one could see was the small black cloud rising above her shapely head.

"A black cloud means bad luck," say the superstitious.

"But wait . . . you can't mean that!"

"Why not?" ask the superstitious, quick to cite another omen: When he was two years old, her older son lost an eye. All the visits to professors in Vienna were in vain, and he wound up with one good eye and one glass eye with a painted brown iris. When he looked closely at something, he turned his head sideways. And her younger son was born prematurely, and for a long time no one knew whether he would survive. Afterward they took him to the professors as well; he was wasted and skinny, his head egg shaped and a little oversize.

"But wait . . . many children are born prematurely, and a lot are stunted or crippled. And these boys were exceptional. The older boy drove his high school teachers to distraction with his questions, and when the younger one was just fourteen he was already poring over Marx. If only they hadn't killed the older one in the forest, and the younger one hadn't died in the camp. . . ."

"Precisely," say the superstitious, and look the other way.

Julia spent two years in the country with her husband and children. They were not well off. Szymon couldn't find work for a long time, so he went to P., where one of his relatives tried to get him work in a large textile firm. Julia and the boys followed him a year later. In P., they were somehow able to make ends meet, and they managed, more or less. But it was obvious that there, too, things were difficult. For when Tulek, the younger boy, was asked, "And what don't you like about living here?" he would answer without hesitation, "The bill collector." Still, Julia immediately became a convert to city life. At what was so very recently pig-feeding time, she now began drinking demitasse cups of black coffee and paying enthusiastic visits to museums and monuments; and every so often she treated herself to a concert. In summer, she sunbathed by the river, but not on the public beaches: she preferred the rocky banks, since they didn't cost anything.

During the second year of her stay in P., two incidents occurred that dramatically cooled her passion for the city she had come to love for its cleanliness and order. Her older son, David, was beaten up by schoolmates who shouted "Get the Jew, get the Jew," and from then on the boy walked hunched over, like someone expecting to be hit.

The second incident took place in the grand concert hall and was equally significant, although more subtle. During the intermission in a famous pianist's recital, Julia heard someone mutter, "Even here there's no getting away from them." She decided to forgo Beethoven's last two sonatas, which she loved so much (intuitively, since she lacked a musical education), and left the concert hall, never to return.

Because many places that year had posted signs that said NO DOGS OR JEWS ALLOWED, the only amusements left were strolls along the river that flowed through the clean, Germanized town. Julia's sons breathed sighs of relief when the school year ended in June and their mother began packing their suitcases for the vacation they were going to spend in her native Z. . . .

Julia's sophisticated incarnation had disappeared; there was no trace of the little black cloud, and the face of her friend, who came all the way from Paris, continued to express amazement and wonder. But what he said had nothing to do with wonder or amazement. Out of the blue he told me that Julia had a hard life. . . . As if I didn't know!

September came, and with it the war; the radio spoke a strange new language of exhortations and abbreviations. The town was crowded with people who were fleeing the Germans. Limousines, full of dignitaries with wives and suitcases and adorned with fluttering red-and-white pennants, raced down the street. The limousines were heading south, raising clouds of dust and universal curiosity. No one seriously believed the Germans would occupy the town.

"They won't get this far," people said.

One evening—and all of them were equally fragrant and starry—Julia's husband, Szymon, arrived, swarthier than usual, unshaven. He had fled on foot and in wagons; his feet were torn and bleeding. He kept repeating, "It's a disaster, a disaster." He talked about trains that departed but failed to arrive, about roads choked with refugees and vehicles, about bombers flying overhead, about people and horses left lying in the fields.

Julia was only half listening as she bustled around the kitchen, got a fire going, put on some soup, and heated a kettle of water for a hot bath. The next day she started looking for a place to live.

The limousines were gone, the radio announcers had fallen silent, the front had come to a standstill, and in the second half of the month the Russian troops crossed the border.

Rumors buzzed through the town: "The Russians are coming. They're coming to help against Hitler." Lying on top of one of the four towers that, once upon a time, protected the princes' castle from Tatar raids, we waited and watched the empty road that led past the pond, with its smooth gray water and gray rushes and reeds. In the distance, high on the opposite bank, we could see the white dome of the Uniate church. We watched the empty road and saw a britchka rumbling along, and in the britchka sat the local squire and mayor of the town, a small, round figure with a drooping gray mustache and wearing high-topped boots. The Polish-Jewish-nobleman mayor was driving out to welcome our deliverers with bread and salt. The sun was setting when the first detachments appeared. Several soldiers jumped down onto the bank of the pond, knelt by the water, washed their hands and faces. "Look," Julia's younger son called out, "they have clean towels!"

The next day, the Polish-Jewish-nobleman mayor and the highest town officials were arrested. No one ever heard from them again.

That night we threw into the river the uniforms of the officers who were hiding here, the shattered remnants of the Polish army. They slept in our dining room, on mattresses. And we children were forbidden to go on walks to the tower.

Julia rented a two-room apartment and furnished it with an odd assortment of furniture—one-of-a-kind pieces, as she put it. She decorated it casually, in her own way. She sewed a colorful throw from old dresses and scattered taffeta pillows on the dilapidated couch. Coarse saddle blankets covered the beds, a peasant bench stood in one corner, and there were wildflowers in unglazed clay jugs. The whole picture was neither town nor country, as she herself was neither citified nor rural. She placed the Parisian sands and Florentine straws in a box and put the box in a wardrobe. She shrugged off her sophisticated style like a worn-out coat, without fussing or complaining. She began to dress a little carelessly, in loose, comfortable clothes. She put on weight.

In the mornings she made noodles, shredded cabbage, did the laundry, patched clothes, but at five o'clock without fail she boiled some ersatz coffee and drank it sitting on her dilapidated couch, surrounded by friends both old and new: Henio from Paris, whom the war had trapped in Z. and who again was whispering about her metamorphosis, was a daily guest; the laundress Antosia came over for a chat; the local history teacher and a tiny, terrified old lady, the court stenographer, were there, as well.

Once a week, on market day, the peasant couple with whom she had once lived in the country would put in an appearance. They came to visit and to get advice. She offered them, as she did all her guests, homemade cookies—underbaked, a little doughy—and coffee in fine porcelain demitasse cups. They would ask, "Why are you so stingy, Auntie? You ought to buy some real mugs; these things can hold just about as much coffee as a cat can cry tears." After which they would seek her advice as to whether it paid to sell their bay horse, who was lame but could still work, or whether Malanka wasn't too old for Stepan. . . . As they left they set a basket covered with a flowered kerchief next to the wall. It contained eggs, cheese, and butter.

"You see," Julia said, "we're not doing badly. That is, we're no worse off than a lot of other people. Maybe even better. You always have to consider those less fortunate. Remember that."

Szymon worked at the mill, and the flour that he received in payment saved them from the shortages that tormented everyone. They ate almost nothing but foods made from flour, and it was no doubt the fault of the dumplings that Julia became so wide and shapeless. Despite her weight she still moved lightly and gracefully. Her heavy fur coat (a gift) tied with a rawhide belt and the wool cap pulled low on her forehead made her look like one of the landowners' wives whom the new authorities had driven off their estates and deported to the east. She smoked cigarettes filled with cheap shag tobacco.

During that first wartime winter she read Montherlant, diligently copying quotations and adding her own comments in the thick notebook in which she also scribbled accounts and shopping lists. Montherlant had been brought from Paris by Henio. She didn't care for him; she missed Proust, who had remained in P. In the evening, at suppertime, when they sat down to their dumplings, fierce arguments erupted. Szymon, a Bundist, jeered, while the younger boy, who was discovering Marx at the time, defended everything that was happening and spoke disdainfully of his older brother as an "aestheticizing liberal."

"And you, Mama? What about you?" they asked. Julia covered her ears with her hands. Once, they forced her to answer, and then she said that she was simply afraid. Of what was happening then and what would happen next.

According to their new passports, issued by the new authorities, they were classified under "paragraph eleven," and from then on they could live only in the provinces, at least one hundred kilometers away from any major city. This paragraph was used to control the so-called unreliable element, which included all the people from the western part of the country who, by fleeing the Germans, had changed their place of residence when the war broke out. The fact that Julia, Szymon, and their children had all been born in Z. meant nothing: to the authorities, they, too, were "refugees."

Szymon greeted the paragraph with a dismissive shrug. Not Julia. She sat on the couch, her plaid peasant shawl wrapped around her, hunched over, worried, not at all herself. She seemed about to say something, then fell silent, took a stocking out of her basket, and began darning.

Her friend Henio jumped up from his chair. "Perhaps I'm in the way . . . you wanted to say something . . . perhaps my presence—"

"My God, don't be such an idiot!" Julia blurted out in her throaty cigarette voice. "Just sit still, will you?"

"I'm sure what she wanted to say was that our passports probably mean we'll be deported to Siberia," Szymon explained.

Behind the gold rims of Henio's glasses, his eyes glittered, blue and frightened. The friend from Paris had recently become as fragile and thin as a twig. He worked as a watchman in a lumberyard. "I'm not complaining," he used to say, "I don't earn much, but I have time to read." Now he was reading the Russians. Julia tried to fatten him up a little with her dumplings.

Julia and Szymon were not deported, but Henio was sent to Siberia in the spring. They managed to bring a sack of dried bread to the station for him. "He'll die there. He's as helpless as a child," Julia said.

"We'll envy him yet," Szymon replied, and later Julia often repeated those words.

But that day she wasn't thinking about deportation, only about David, her older son. She was thinking that their passports made it impossible for him to enter the university.

"I know," she said, "it's stupid of me. I feel terribly sorry for the boy. He's so capable . . . he dreamed of going to the university. It's a great blow."

"What do you mean 'great blow'?" Szymon snapped as if he'd been scalded. "Don't use words like that about this!"

On the day of David's departure for the isolated village there was a fierce blizzard and severe frost. The sleigh stopped in front of the house. Sheepskins, smiles, shouts. Julia in her enormous coat, holding a shag cigarette. David climbed clumsily onto the sleigh; his schoolmates, boys and girls, were already seated. Like him, they were going to the isolated village, except with a different purpose. They were taking the sleigh to the village station in order to board the long-distance express train that inexplicably stopped for a minute in that remote place. Usually, no one got on there and no one got off; nobody knew for whom the express stopped. David's schoolmates would board the train calmly, avoiding a crush and without having to fight the crowds of travelers who were besieging the station in town. They were returning from their semester vacation; in a few days their new term would start.

The same sleigh would then take David to a one-room schoolhouse. He had accepted a position as teacher in the isolated village. But for now he sat among the fortunate ones, wrapped in his enormous sheepskin. He turned his head to one side and looked at his mother.

"Did you pack Tacitus?" he asked, and Julia nodded.

"What about *The Red and the Black*?"

"That too," said Julia in her smoky voice.

And David said, "I'll be back at Easter, when the snow melts."

The snow drifted down; huge, dry flakes tumbled out of the sky. The sleigh took off without a sound. For a moment one could still hear laughter and shouts, and then only silence, grayness, white.

"Profession?" an SS man would soon ask.

"Teacher," David would reply, and with that answer would seal his fate.

June 1941 was almost over; the Germans were already in the town. The synagogue had been burned down, the beards of the pious Jews had been cut off, the stores had been looted, the shoemaker shot on the stool where he sat with his hammer in his hand, and nine other Jews had been shot, too. Flapping above the main street were blue-and-yellow signs that said in Ukrainian LONG LIVE A FREE UKRAINE! Blue and yellow ribbons decorated the jackets of Ukrainians who welcomed Hitler and whose reward was the freedom to do whatever they liked for three days, the right to stage a pogrom. Windows were closed, doors barred. From nearby towns came news of burned synagogues, of Jews dragged from their houses and shot. After three days of freedom to do whatever they liked, there was silence. The town broke out in a rash of white posters, orders, and prohibitions all repeating the word *Tod.*

June turned into July; the linden trees perfumed the air; the frogs croaked in the river; the dogs bayed at the moon; the nights were bright and sleepless. The white posters demanded tribute. The Jews gathered gold and silver, coffee and tea, and money, money. The *Landrat* insisted on silver tableware and valuable china. From nearby towns came news of gold and silver, of coffee and tea and money, money. Gold and silver, coffee and tea, were supposed to buy peace and quiet in the town, peace that was not peace, quiet that was not quiet.

"People are naive," Szymon shouted, "whoever believes them is naive. This is only the prelude," he shouted, "only the beginning." He did not say what it was the beginning of. He didn't have to.

Julia, Szymon, and the boys were now living with us. On the first day of the German occupation, they moved from their centrally located apartment to our house, hidden in the gardens of a quiet backstreet. They occupied the former nursery that now was empty and furnished it only with what was necessary for day-to-day existence. The walls were bare; the room was bare. The green leaves outside the windows and the towering Castle Hill were the only ornaments. Julia, always so handy at decorating an interior with whatever was available, didn't bother this time. The pillows, the kilims, the pitchers—she left everything in her old apartment. She took the beds, a table, four chairs, and a wardrobe. That was all. She had simply alighted for a moment in passing.

The time when we lived together under the same roof has left little trace of her; she remains invisible. Here and there I can find some meaningless bits that have lodged in my memory for no apparent reason. I see her sitting on a bench in the garden, under the cherry tree, a pince-nez on her nose, an unread book on her knees. I hear her asking if things are quiet in town. Or she's warming kasha in the kitchen, and Agafia is giving her the evil eye; Agafia doesn't like intruders in her kingdom. (So those bits must be from the first few weeks, since Agafia was still reigning in the kitchen; they hadn't yet forbidden her to reign over a Jewish household.) The peasant couple from the village came less and less frequently and soon stopped appearing altogether. Another bit, from a later time: Julia and I are walking down the street and suddenly a car, an open black limousine, speeds past, the black limousine of the *Landrat.* A few strands of blond hair have blown across the face of Slavka, the daughter of the Ukrainian priest—her pale face with its fine features and the haughty, superior smile on her thin lips.

"David was in love with her," Julia said suddenly. David was already dead by then. We hadn't known he was in love with Slavka. She was a girl who was at first very fat and then became very thin. The *Landrat*'s mistress. Always dressed in black, always with her fine windblown hair. I remember that scene as if from a film: the black hull of the open car, the black-clothed figure of the pale girl, her hair the color of wheat. And I hear Julia's smoky voice.

David died two months after the Germans invaded; he was shot in a nearby forest. After the war Julia went to the forest and, following the directions the peasants had given her, located the execution site. It was a small clearing, near the edge of the woods, surrounded by young oaks and hazels. Lush green grass carpeted the ground. Julia said that the peasants called her attention to the exceptional beauty of the grass in this spot.

Several months later Tulek was deported. They caught him at dawn; he was rushing with his spade over his shoulder to work on the Ostbahn. Julia had handed him the spade herself, yelling at him to hurry up. She had been torn from sleep by the cry, *"Aktion!"* Her feet bare, her hair disheveled, her face distraught, she had handed her son the spade she thought could be his salvation. You'll be safe there . . . hurry. . . . And then she watched as her younger boy, her tall, thin, fifteen-year-old boy, ran down the leafy street and disappeared around the corner.

That evening she lay on her bed, listless, covered with a brown blanket. Like a clod of earth. Szymon hissed, "Leave us alone." We tiptoed out of the room. The black garden, the black hill, dead silence on the street, all the houses dark and deserted. Dogs were barking on the other side of the river on that black summer night.

All that Tulek left behind were two notes smuggled out of the Janowski camp. In the first, he asked for a warm sweater; in the second, for poison. After Julia's death, we found those notes in a carved box from Zakopane, locked with a tiny key. Along with the notes was a schoolboy's notebook, filled with large, crooked writing that reminded us of Tulek's thin, crooked body. Part of a diary. Tulek wrote about his deep, unrequited love for a girl named Ludka. We couldn't recall who that was.

Later, in the ghetto, Julia adopted an orphan girl, so that there were four of them who sought shelter at the miller's house beside the pond. Szymon's old father, who had survived by accident and later died of old age in their hiding place, was with them. They buried him in the courtyard, at night, in secret, afraid of dogs and neighbors. It was winter, and the earth was frozen.

They sat in the attic for a year, and only the miller knew they were there. Julia taught the girl to read and write, and

Szymon helped her memorize the multiplication tables. In the hideout, the girl started calling Julia "Mama."

The day after liberation, Szymon contracted typhus. Strong, stocky Szymon survived to the end and died during the first week of freedom. Julia said that she had foreseen everything, and that when Szymon was burning with fever she knew it would be her adopted daughter's turn next. She nursed her husband and the child in the hope that she herself would fall ill. "You don't survive typhus twice," said Szymon during a fleeting moment of consciousness. He had already survived typhus during the first war. The little girl died one week after he did. Delirious with fever, Julia called for her sons. It was March 1944.

"I know everything about her," Henio exclaimed, Henio from Paris, who had returned safely from Russia. "Everything . . ." The same blue eyes, the same wisps on his head. I had never seen Henio cry.

"Niobe," he whispered. "Niobe."

Next to him stood a slight woman with short sprightly legs. She asked sternly, "Do you want your blood pressure to shoot up again?" and Henio obediently stopped crying.

"If it weren't for her," he said in a confidential whisper, "I would have croaked from hunger." (So he had changed after all; the word "croaked" would not have passed his lips before.) And again he whispered, right in my ear now, with admiration in his voice, "Just imagine, she hasn't read a single book in her entire life."

The little woman with the sprightly legs was Henio's wife. They were waiting to leave for America.

Julia, resettled from the former eastern borderlands to what had become the western ones, worked as a book-keeper in a marmalade factory. The region was beautiful, untouched by the war; every town had an old market-place, old arcades, old fountains, everything picture perfect, forests and hills all around, and among the forests and hills was one spa after another. Chopin himself once took the waters and gave a concert in one of these spas. Few people knew about the small camps that had been scattered about there—the so-called *Nebenlager*—and those who did know were silent.

In the aftermath of war and forced evacuations, crowds of people swarmed through the courtyards, looting was commonplace, and the vodka flowed in streams. Every evening in the pub known as Pod Jeleniem—Under the Hart—a pianist played "Red Poppies from Monte Cassino." The hair was just beginning to grow back on his shaved head. The woman who managed the restaurant had survived the war with forged papers, the pianist had been in Auschwitz, and the buxom waitresses in the clinging black dresses used to serve beer here when the Führer looked down from the wall and the place was called Zum Hirschen.

Beyond the third spa lay the border, supposedly open because it had not yet been hermetically sealed, just partially closed off. Whoever wanted to leave had better hurry.

Julia accompanied Henio to the school building that

served as a billet for the Jews who were leaving the country that had become their loved ones' cemetery. "Take care," she said. Henio wiped his tear-stained glasses; all day long he was wiping his glasses.

"He'll be all right, Julia," his wife replied, "I'll take care of him. He just has to learn a trade. My brother-in-law has a tailor shop over there."

Henio just kept on repeating, "Niobe . . ."

Julia worked as a bookkeeper in a marmalade factory. She collected demitasse cups and immediately gave them away as gifts; she collected colorful ceramics, buttons, and silk cloth for sewing. She assembled a lovely collection of buttons. She toured the countryside, hiked through the green hills, rode out to the destroyed town to look at the ruined churches on the island and the various bridges. She had placed a seal of silence over her own past. She mothered young people, and the young clung to her. They called her Auntie.

"When I recovered from typhus, I told myself, Live or die. And as you see, I am alive. And that means I have obligations." A moment later, she added, "At least outside, in the world."

But what was she like when she shut her apartment door behind her in the evening? Szymon's glances followed her as she moved about the room, and her boys' carefree laughter echoed from the walls. They were standing on the bridge in Z. David was carrying a book; Tulek was holding a ball. The water babbled merrily under the bridge.

People wrote from Israel, from the United States, from Australia. She didn't want to go abroad. Why? For whom? It was a long time before she packed her suitcases.

No one knew yet that the year of her arrival would be the year of a war counted in days, nor that the other time—the time that swallowed up her boys and Szymon and was sealed and double locked with silence—would couple with the time of the present war to rip open the floodgates, releasing the full violence of that wave that would strike her tired, sick heart.

No one knew this yet, and Julia was diligently, laboriously studying the foreign alphabet and foreign phrases. In the evening she sat on a school bench; during the day she opened her notebook over and over. . . . No one foresaw anything yet as Julia renewed old friendships and made new ones, as she traveled to the sea to watch the sunset, sat under a sycamore tree and wrote letters.

There wasn't a single cloud in the sky, and the days were getting warmer. No one foresaw anything yet, and what still awaited Julia was a meeting with the elderly friend of her youth, who, like so many others, would come here for Passover and sit on the hotel terrace with its view of the gray sea and with the parching winds blowing across it. Bald, blue-eyed, wearing a checked jacket, a tie with a palm-tree pattern, he would tell Julia, "I'm reading the Americans now."

"And during the day he sews trousers," his wife would add. "He's a good tailor."

Julia smoked a cigarette, looked at the sea (she loved the sea), and recited in Hebrew, in her hoarse voice, the first sentence of the schoolbook for immigrants: "*Yam, bayam oniyah* . . .the sea, on the sea a ship . . ."

Only as the end of May approached and the days became even hotter, and the parching winds blew even more fiercely, would history rapidly unfold. The news announcers repeated in every language: The Strait of Tiran is closed; the UN forces have been recalled. . . . Escalation, escalation.

Tanks waiting on the Negev sands. Days of anxious waiting.

Huddled over an atlas, Julia breathed heavily. "The ghetto," she said, "the ghetto before an *Aktion* . . . save the children."

She demanded that the radio be tuned to Cairo and that the reports broadcast in Hebrew be translated for her. "How do you know they won't do it?" she asked. "No one believed anything then either. Look," she opened the atlas, "take a look. We're a tiny point on the map."

And again, "The children . . . the children . . ."

In the evening we sat on the balcony. The air smelled of tangerines; helicopters were buzzing high overhead; airplanes were moving heavily across the sky. Julia placed her hand on her chest and said: Give me my medicine.

The attack came just after the cease-fire, in the early morning. The ambulance raced through the city enveloped in the peaceful, deep sleep of relief. As she lay in bed in the hospital, she asked to hear the radio announcements.

She never opened her eyes after the second attack; she was dozing. She seemed to shrink and flatten out. Just once she stirred and—completely coherent—asked in her smoky voice, loudly, clearly, "Has the UN already held its general meeting? What is Kosygin saying?"

That same night she saw her sons and called them to her.

In the little carved box mentioned above, where we found the two notes smuggled out of the Janowski camp and Tulek's diary, we also found a few pictures. One of them shows Julia with her arms around both boys. She is slender, elegant, wearing gloves that reach her elbows.

Her head is bent over, her face hidden by the black wings of a broad straw hat.

THE BAKER'S ONGOING RESURRECTION

For weeks now they've been bringing the baker Weiskranz back to life, only to kill him again, always in the same ingenious way. They start off with a brief topographical description, just to give the lay of the land, and proceed with their version of the baker's last moments. The accuracy of the account depends on the memory of each teller.

Among those, for example, who mention the flat cement structure at the back of the camp, there are some who refer to it as a "pool." This implies that the structure was not built for the sole purpose of drowning prisoners who were so weak that when they were tossed inside and made to lie in the shallow water they simply drowned. Others, however, maintain that this "pool" was designed expressly for that purpose. Still others have no idea of its existence.

It's the same with the shed. Many assume it was used to store shovels, wheelbarrows, and pickaxes, but there are those who are quick to add that it also served to store the bodies of people who had been murdered. For others the tool room is shrouded in the fog of forgetfulness.

And it's the same with Weiskranz, with one difference: everybody knows how he was murdered, and many saw it with their own eyes.

Day after day new details keep filling in the first rough sketch, but in the end certain parts remain completely blank: In which direction did the barrel roll with the baker inside it? Down the length of the square or across it? Did it stop when it ran into the wire fence, or did the prisoners stop it when the commandant ordered them to?

Of course these are not the only blank frames in this painstakingly assembled montage about dying in a barrel. There are more such imprecisions, which is why, during a bright hot summer many, many years after the tragic but at that time commonplace event, baker Weiskranz is forced to rise from the dead and die again, day after day.

And both resurrection and death occur in slow motion; the camera notes every detail, even the most banal—it was about to rain; the farmers were raking hay—and every phase of the event itself.

It's five in the morning. The month of September. To find the exact date we would have to consult the Jewish calendar, since we're speaking about a Jewish holiday.

Barracks number 2. There are only ten barracks; the camp isn't very big.

It's five in the morning, and in the camp a new day is dawning.

No sooner has the day dawned than the accounts begin to diverge.

Some narrators claim that on that day Weiskranz did

not get up from his cot himself but was awoken by Kapo Heinz, who was inspecting the barracks and discovered the sick baker on top of his straw mattress and a bottle underneath. And that Heinz immediately reported the offense to the commandant. As far as the bottle is concerned, everyone agrees that it existed: Weiskranz had an infected bladder; he didn't have the strength to get up during the night. The discrepancies have to do with the timing. Did Kapo Heinz discover it on the same day that Weiskranz was murdered? That is, was the barrel a direct result of the bottle?

There are many who say: Yes. Absolutely. I remember exactly.

But there are also many who say that the incident with the bottle happened a week earlier, that the barrel has nothing to do with the bottle discovered by Heinz, that the barrel happened later.

Some say: It was five in the morning. At five we would get up to be counted. Kapo Heinz burst into the barracks, calling out *Aufstehen Kinder!*—wake up children, time for breakfast!—so everyone knew that Kapo Heinz had gotten up on the wrong side of bed. And everyone tried to sneak out of the barracks as quickly as possible, but not everyone succeeded, since Heinz was standing at the entrance doling out his "breakfast" with his stick, hitting this one on the head, and that one. . . .

Afterward he inspected the barracks, which he didn't always do, and that's when he discovered the old baker Weiskranz, wrapped up in a blanket, lying on a lower bunk in the corner. He had been sick for several days. Benio, the barracks elder, hadn't reported Weiskranz, since Benio wasn't a bad guy and did what he could. But there wasn't much he could do. So Kapo Heinz was standing over Weiskranz, and old Weiskranz, already a Muselmann, was fast asleep.

Well, we said to ourselves, now you see him; now you don't. Today there's Weiskranz, but once Heinz hits him with his stick that will be that. However, the first thing Kapo Heinz did was bend over and take the bottle out from underneath the bunk. Weiskranz didn't have the strength to get up during the night and go to the bucket. It was only then that the kapo started yelling. He forgot all about using the stick and ran off to tell the commandant.

Kapo Heinz was—as everyone knows—the dog in charge of all the other dogs. The barracks elder, Benio, said to the baker: Weiskranz, you better get up and go to the boilers, because I can't cover for you anymore. So Weiskranz pulled himself off his bunk and marched off to sift coal at the *Kohlensieberei*, where the commandant showed up at ten o'clock along with the head kapo. They dragged him to the square and ordered him to crawl inside the barrel.

Still others say: He was an elderly man, very pious. He worked in the *Kohlensieberei*, and within a month he had already turned into a Muselmann, since it was very hard labor. Benio, the barracks elder, covered for him, because Benio had a very pious father whom they had gassed in the main camp. Benio often said that Weiskranz reminded him of his father. That was the only reason he protected him, because usually Benio wasn't so nice. And then, when Kapo

Heinz found the bottle underneath the baker's bed, Benio had a talk with Heinz, and the kapo didn't report it to the commandant. Weiskranz, weak and sick as he was, got up and went to the *Kohlensieberei* in order to avoid the infirmary—because if he wound up in the infirmary they would take him to the main camp, to the ovens. It wasn't until a week later that they killed him on the square, in the barrel. For a completely different reason . . .

Every morning, and these summer days are brighter and hotter than that day in September, the baker lies dozing on his bunk. Every day Kapo Heinz enters barracks number 2 and says the same thing about breakfast. Day after day he inspects the barracks, day after day the sick baker pulls himself from his bed and, supported by the other prisoners, stands on the square to be counted. . . .

For a completely different reason, they say, and not until a week later. Benio was able to buy him out of the bottle business. But a week later the feeble, sick baker Weiskranz pulled himself from his bunk in the morning, went around the barracks, and told the prisoners it was a day of fasting. He didn't line up for coffee in the morning. He was very pious and God-fearing; he fasted and wanted the others to fast as well. But no one fasted, only him. He could barely stand on his feet and the commandant noticed that at once. Then Kapo Heinz told the commandant that the prisoner was weak because he was fasting, and the commandant looked around the square and pointed to the empty lime barrel.

"In das Fass hinein!"—"Into the barrel!"—he shouted. The head kapo stuffed Weiskranz into the barrel and ordered

it to be rolled around the square, which dropped off toward the wire fence, beyond which flowed the river.

Others say: The commandant himself put him in the barrel and ordered the barrel to be rolled from the watch-tower across the square.

Some say: They rolled the barrel for five minutes.

Some say: Ten minutes.

The commandant shouted: *"Genug!"*

The head kapo shouted: *"Genug!"*

All agree: When the barrel stopped rolling Weiskranz was no longer alive.

All agree: Everything happened between ten and eleven in the morning.

All agree: It was about to rain. In the field beyond the wire fence the farmers were raking hay.

For weeks now they've been bringing baker Weiskranz back to life, only to kill him again, always in the same ingenious way. Every morning, Kapo Heinz bursts into barracks number 2; every morning the baker pulls himself from his bunk. Every morning, a thousand kilometers away, the commandant climbs down from the second floor of his three-bedroom house and raises the blinds of the shop in which he sells smoked meat; the head kapo sits down at his desk at the automobile company.

Neither of them has ever heard of baker Weiskranz, who for many more months, and maybe even years, will keep rising from the dead and dying in the barrel.